Wine Sisters Forever

Jan Romes

WINE AND SWEAT PANTS SERIES BOOK 5

Wine Sisters Forever
Wine and Sweat Pants Series – Book 5
Copyright © 2019 Janice Romes
All Rights Reserved

Cover Design and Formatting by Tugboat Design
www.tugboatdesign.net

This book is licensed for your personal enjoyment only. This book may not be resold or given away to other people. If you would like to share this book with another person, please purchase an additional copy for each recipient. If you're reading this book and did not purchase it, or if it was not purchased for your use only then please purchase your own copy. Thank you for respecting the hard work of this author.

This is a work of fiction. Names, characters, places and incidents are either the product of the author's imagination or are used fictitiously, and any resemblance to actual persons, living or dead, events, or locales is entirely coincidental.

Dedicated to my husband:

His unyielding confidence in me is amazing! He still makes me laugh and his quirkiness has rubbed off on me after all these years. How could it not? Part of Elaina, Tawny, Steph, and Grace's humorous personalities can be indirectly blamed on him and part comes from my mom and my siblings.

Hugs to:

My kids, daughter-in-law, son-in-law, and grandkids.

Special thanks to:

Sharon Stienecker
Rachel Kleister
The FJ Wine Warrior Ladies
Deborah Bradseth
Friends, family, and fellow authors

Dear Readers:

I can't believe I'm at book #5 in this series. Scenes of chaos, drama, and friendship for Elaina, Tawny, Steph, and Grace continue to play out in my head. These incredible women have been through a lot already, but their journeys aren't quite finished. Elaina had and possibly still has something going on with Jess. In Wine Club Wednesdays, she confessed strong feelings for him and even used the L-word. He brushed it off with humor and went back to the state of Virginia to help his daughter through a critical time in her life. As the saga goes forth, we'll see if those strong feelings remain in Elaina and whether they can sustain a long-distance relationship. The light burned out for Tawny and Bart. Steph and Nicholas have a lot in common, so they're still doing well. Grace and Philip have a sweet thing going on, and they bought a fixer-upper, eighteenth-century Victorian house together.

What these four women have found as they've grown individually and also together as best friends, is how different and challenging life can be as a single person. They're guiding me through the rest of their stories and I'll be guiding you through them. There will be some tender moments and many dramatic ones as well. Of course, they wouldn't allow me to shortchange them, or you, on the fun.

Packed in this book you'll see a ton of resistance, theatrics, spectacular development, a lot of weirdness and humor; and more than anything, an exorbitant amount of love — the kind between soul mates and true friends.

I'd be remiss if I failed to mention Stony the adorable Husky, Lula the feisty feline, and Bailey the tiny Pomsky. These three animal friends add to the joy and confusion.

Grab a glass of wine or other beverage of choice, kick back and get ready for all that these crazy characters have to offer.

Thank you for staying with this series and with me as an author.

Love to all of you,
Jan

Wine Sisters Forever

Chapter One

~ *Girls Night Out!* ~

"It's Wednesday – our girl's night – and you ordered water? I can't wrap my head around that, Tawn'." Grace used her tongue to collect salt from the rim of her margarita glass.

Tawny swirled the ice around in the tall glass of H2O and shrugged. "I don't drink enough water."

"We may have to kick you out of the wine club."

Tawny lowered her long eyelashes over her eyes. "Just try, ya little pip squeak."

Elaina and Steph made faint noises of disapproval at the back and forth taunting that had been on-going most of the day.

"Tawny's slacking. Let me see a show of hands. Who thinks we should oust her from the club?" Grace shot her arm in the air.

Elaina smirked. "No one's getting kicked out of anything."

Steph clanged her fork on her plate to get their

attention. "You're a good one to spout off, Grace. We're a wine club and you're having a margarita. Ease up on the heckling. A little bit goes a long way."

A grin spread across Grace's face at Steph's reprimand. "I'm just giving her chain a good yank."

Tawny walked her fingers across the table. "Keep it up and I'll be yanking something of yours real soon too. How attached are you to those eyebrows?"

"Ert!"

"I'll ert you." Tawny grabbed the basket of dinner rolls, making Grace flinch. "Yeah, that's what I thought. You fear me."

"Bahaha! Funniest thing I've heard this century."

Steph nibbled on the end a shrimp from her stir-fry. She'd been trying new techniques when it came to her eating habits. Her goal was to still enjoy good food, but to eat less. This week's method involved enjoying food at a turtle pace. At the rate she was going, it would be midnight before she finished. Regardless, Elaina was in awe of Steph's determination to achieve the svelte figure she so desired. Their waitress had delivered their orders twenty-five minutes ago, and Steph's plate still looked full. Tawny's plate gave the appearance it hadn't been touched either. Elaina hadn't noticed until now that everything Tawny had ordered was bland – baked white fish, mashed potatoes with no gravy, and green beans. Mild food, ice water, and eating just a few bites could only mean one thing – another serious bout of heartburn was messing with her. Poor gal was fighting Grace *and* indigestion.

Their waitress returned to the table. "How are we doing here?"

"Mostly good. Would you happen to have a set of eyebrow pliers in the kitchen?"

"Tweezers?"

"Tweezers, pliers, whatever – as long as they're industrial grade and made of steel alloy with jaws strong enough to..."

Grace motioned to Tawny with her thumb. "Don't mind her. She's had a little too much water. We should've cut her off two glasses ago."

Tawny poked Grace's hand with her fork.

"See what I mean? Too much water makes her violent."

Tawny pressed the tines harder.

"All right already. You've made your point. I'll stop bugging you. Geez. Get a grip."

"I'll get a great grip...with a set of pliers."

Elaina smiled up at the waitress. "They really are good friends. Hard to tell, I know."

The waitress made a wise decision not to weigh in. "Can I interest anyone in dessert?"

Someone sitting a few tables away drew everyone's interest with a series of loud, broken coughs.

Steph stretched to see over Elaina. "He may have a chicken bone lodged in his throat."

Tawny swiveled around to survey the scene. In a blink, she was out of her chair. Elaina, Steph, Grace, and the waitress ran to assist.

"Sir, I'm here to help," Tawny said to get his permission.

The man's eyes were glazed over and he continued to cough. One of his two table mates whacked him on the back, which did nothing because he wasn't actually choking.

Tawny knelt to bring herself eye to eye with the guy in distress. "Shellfish allergy?"

He confirmed her suspicion with a jerky nod.

"That doesn't make sense." One of the men at the table explained that Kace had eaten steak, not seafood.

Tawny scanned the remnants of food on their plates. "Did either of you offer him anything from your plate?"

"I gave him my broccoli, why?"

"The broccoli might've touched your shrimp and lobster." Tawny calmly told Elaina to call 9-1-1 and then asked the coughing man if he kept an epinephrine pen on hand.

The poor guy's face was strained and his lips had swelled. Between coughs, he managed to squeak out, "In..."

Urgency, and possibly panic, seized Tawny and she fired a question at his friends. "Did he drive here?"

"Kace's black Cadillac is in the first row of the parking lot."

She snapped her fingers. "Keys. I need keys."

The two men stood their friend up to get the keys out of his pocket.

Tawny tossed them to Steph. "Check his glove compartment and console for an epinephrine pen. Run, Steph."

Steph dashed away, bobbing and weaving through

the maze of tables until she was out of sight.

Tawny doled out duties like a boss. She told the manager to wait outside for the rescue squad and to guide the EMTs inside. Grace was instructed to corral onlookers at their tables. Elaina's job entailed keeping a clear path for Steph's return.

The path-clearing order came too late. Steph was already on her way back and almost mowed over a waiter with a full tray of food propped on his shoulder. In the last second before impact, both she and the waiter managed to sidestep each other. In another amazing feat, the waiter held the tray steady, and no plates crashed to the floor.

Out of breath, Steph thrust the medicine pen into Tawny's waiting hands.

Tawny knelt again. "Do I have your consent to use the pen?"

Watching Tawny in action was amazing. In the emergency room, there was no doubt she would've already used the pen since the patient's presence there meant he or she had come seeking help. This gentleman, however, was in public. Before proceeding, she'd given him an opportunity to refuse her assistance.

Kace's face and neck had become a red welt zone. He frantically moved his head.

Emergency sirens could be heard coming ever closer.

Tawny removed the cap and pressed the orange part of the pen firmly against the guy's thigh until it clicked.

The medication seemed to kick in almost immediately. Kace's coughing didn't cease, but it lessened, and his wheezing in between coughs stopped altogether.

Rotating red lights shone through the windows and bounced from wall to wall. The driver of the ambulance cut the siren. Two EMTs rushed on scene with a medical bag and gurney.

Tawny explained the situation and that she'd administered epinephrine.

After checking Kace's vitals, it was determined his condition was severe enough to warrant another dose. From their bag, they produced the much needed drug. One of the EMTs hurriedly scribbled down Tawny's name and number. They strapped Kace onto the gurney, and in a matter of minutes, he was on his way to the hospital.

An aftermath of shock hit them all, most especially Tawny. She stumbled back to their table and practically dropped into her chair. She'd broken out in a sweat and her hands were trembling.

Elaina patted her arm. "You did great, Tawn'. Can I get you another glass of water?"

Tawny clutched the edge of the table. "Forget the water. Bring me wine."

* * *

"Within a minute you knew what had to be done and shoved that needle into his thigh like you were a doctor." Steph slurred her words. "Y-you're my hero, T-tawnster."

Elaina had loaded her glass with ice cubes to dilute the wine. They'd been celebrating Tawny's heroic act for almost three hours and enjoying the fact that tonight was all about them. Lately, either bed and breakfast guests, or Philip and Nicholas took the bulk of their time, which was great; yet they'd longed for some four-on-four time. Today they were guest-free, and the guys had been ordered not to horn in on Wine Club Wednesday.

"I hope Kace is okay." Tawny kept looking over her shoulder as though she expected him to walk back into the restaurant.

Steph topped off all their glasses with more wine. "You saved his life."

"Do you think Kace is his given name?" Tawny tipped her wine glass back and forth, and seemed mesmerized by the 'legs' that ran down the inside of the glass.

Elaina offered a suggestion. "Let's find out."

"His friends left shortly after the ambulance took off, so we'd have no way to extract that information."

"I meant make a call. You have connections at the hospital."

"I can't inquire due to patient privacy."

Grace removed her phone from the pocket of her jean jacket. "What's the hospital's main phone number?"

"No, Grace."

"Yes, Tawny." Grace corrected it to, "Tawnster."

"I'd rather none of you call me by that name. It sounds like a combination of Tawny and monster." Tawny made a fist and pressed it into her solar plexus. "Dang heartburn. I took some antacids before we came."

Grace's blue eyes glistened with mischief. "Let's take her to the hospital. Maybe we'll run into Kace."

Elaina's gaze remained fixed on Tawny. "It might be a good idea, Tawn'. Not to locate Kace, but to get you some serious relief. Your heartburn episodes are becoming more frequent."

"Don't be ridiculous. I'm not going to the hospital for heartburn. I'll pay a visit to my family physician soon."

Elaina narrowed her eyes. "I so want to boss you right now."

"I know you do." Tawny motioned for their waitress.

The woman came to the table in a rush. "More wine?"

"We've had great food, wine, and service. We've also had a sideshow that included an ambulance. It's time to bring this spectacular and unusual night to a close. Do you have our bills ready?"

"Yes, ma'am."

Grace insisted on paying for the meals. They squawked, but gave in to her generosity.

Outside, Steph grabbed Grace's arm. "Uh oh." She swayed and laughed.

Elaina felt slightly tipsy too. "I'm right there with you, Steph."

Grace boasted that she wasn't alcohol impaired.

"Right." Tawny directed their attention to a vacant parking space marked with white paint. "Prove you can walk a straight line."

"I'm able to walk that line blindfolded and on one foot."

Tawny's eyebrows lifted high. "Five bucks says you can't." She slapped a five dollar bill on the hood of her car.

"Make it ten and I'll do it."

"Fine. Ten bucks, it is." Tawny rubbed her hands together. "Now to blindfold you." She removed the knitted scarf from around her neck.

Grace crossed her arms. "Go ahead. Tie me up."

Tawny wrapped the scarf around Grace's eyes and knotted it in the back of her head. She put a finger to her lips to shush Elaina and Steph, and snapped Grace's picture with her phone. "It's time to walk the talk... literally...and on one foot."

Grace hopped on one foot and teetered to the left. Elaina put out her arms to catch Grace.

A round of laughter hit the cool April air.

"Blindfolded or not, none of us are in any shape to drive home. I'm getting us a ride." Elaina tapped an app on her phone and made arrangements.

Tawny hiccupped. "Even if we weren't half-lit, we'd need a car to pick us up. On the way here, I feared my beloved Ferdinand was going to take his last breath."

"You've taken great care of your car, but the odometer says it's time for a new one." Steph smoothed a hand over the Malibu's roof.

"The odometer?" Tawny scoffed. "More like the engine. Poor Ferdie hasn't been right for a month."

Grace jammed her hands on her hips. "I offered to drive tonight. You insisted we take your car."

"You should also point out that her night vision stinks." Elaina knew she'd be the recipient of a glare. To her surprise, Tawny shrugged and emitted a whimper.

"I suppose I'm in denial that both Ferdie and I need some TLC."

* * *

Seated beside Tawny in the taxi cab, Elaina whispered, "Do you regret giving Bart the heave-ho?"

"What? No. Why would you even ask?"

"You said you're in need of TLC."

Quincy, their driver, looked in the rearview mirror. Obviously when you speak quietly in a confined space, your words still reach all ears.

"I do need some TLC, just not from Bart. We had one thing in common – our love for animals. It wasn't enough. I need more."

Elaina cast her fishing line. "More what?"

"Everything."

"Too vague. Try again."

Tawny's forehead creased into a frown. "When did you turn into a badger-er?"

"Badger-er?"

"Don't correct my grammar."

This time Quincy didn't just hawk-eye them in the mirror, he also smiled. Elaina was tempted to tell him to keep his eyes on the road. "I'm not *badgering* nor nagging you. I may come across that way, but it's not my objective."

"I thought I was the one living in denial," Tawny spouted.

"Caring and nagging are two very different traits."

Tawny lifted her shoulder in a half-shrug. "You're a caring nag."

Steph peeked over the headrest. "Better a nag than a hag."

Quincy cracked up laughing.

Grace diverted the commentary. "Quincy, did you know you have a Florence Nightingale in your car?"

"I wasn't aware."

"Tawny saved a guy's life tonight."

Tawny released a lengthy moan.

Quincy's congenial manner turned to one of concern. "Is she all right?"

"She's fine. She just hates when we call her a Nightingale. She also hates when we call her Tawnster, but that's a whole other story."

A louder moan alluded to something more than Tawny being irritated by both names. A second later, she grabbed her stomach. "I'm going to throw up."

Quincy pumped the brakes and pulled to the side of the road.

Near a Moose Xing sign, Elaina held Tawny's hair while she got sick.

Between intermittent bouts of vomiting, Tawny shed a few tears. Finally, she placed a shaky hand on Elaina's arm. "I think I'm done."

Wrong. She wasn't finished. Her belly must've decided it like doing gymnastics. It tossed, flipped, and took a spill several times.

Fifteen minutes later, Tawny stood on rubbery legs. She took a step and almost fell. Elaina slung Tawny's arm around her neck and she carefully guided them back to the car.

"Quincy, take us to the hospital."

The wobbly brown-eyed mule, that could barely stand let alone argue, issued the opposite order. "I want to go home."

Quincy's eyes ricocheted between Elaina and Tawny.

"Sorry to put you in the middle of this, Quincy. There's an extra fifty in it for you, if you take us to the hospital."

Tears leaked from the corners of Tawny's eyes. "I'm totally fine." Another round of stomach disturbance erupted from her like a fountain, barely missing the car. The pigheadedness didn't wane. "I'm totally..."

"You're totally going to the hospital."

* * *

Doctor Martin shook hands all around. "You did the right thing by insisting Ms. Westerfield come here."

Elaina crossed her arms. "We practically had to stage a kidnapping."

The doc's mouth curled into a smile. "Health professionals, including myself, oftentimes are the last to admit we need care." He modestly cleared his throat. "Ms. Westerfield's gallbladder is a mess. It's inflamed to the point that I have no choice but to perform a cholecystectomy."

Grace rubbed her forehead. "I don't know what that is, but take care of our friend."

"I'll be removing her gallbladder."

Steph sifted air through her teeth. "Will it improve

her cranky disposition?"

"Given her current condition, I'd say her post-surgery behavior could improve."

Grace looked in every direction. "The coast is clear. Go ahead and say she won't be so..."

Steph put up a palm. "Don't say bitchy, Grace."

The physician's light expression morphed to semi-serious before changing to amusement. "With friends like you, I'd say Ms. Westerfield will be back to her old self in no time."

"I'm telling her you called her old."

Bluish-gray eyes widened. "That's not what I meant."

Elaina quietly told Grace to ease up.

"Sorry, Doc, when I'm nervous I can't seem to stop the flow of nonsense."

"Then you must be nervous 24/7," Steph interjected.

Grace gave Steph mean eyes and then offered a big smile to the kind doctor. "Tawny will be none the wiser that you called her a geezer." She pretended to lock her lips and throw away the key.

"I should've waited until after surgery to speak with you."

Grace flipped out of heckle-mode. "In all seriousness, we've been worried about her. She hasn't felt good for a while. We're thankful you came out to fill us in and that you'll be removing that nasty gallbladder."

Elaina had to ask, "I'm curious. Did she consent to the surgery?"

"No. Yes. No. Yes. No. Yes. Those were her exact words." The doc grinned. "It was touch and go for a little bit. One big stabbing pain convinced her to keep it at yes." Doctor Martin checked his watch. "I'll update you once she's in recovery." He disappeared between the double doors that separated the emergency rooms from the waiting area.

Steph wandered back to her chair. "We need a do-over on Girls Night."

Elaina took the adjacent seat. "Why? We had a great meal and plenty of fermented-grape. Tawny rescued someone in trouble. Her heartburn issues are about to end. We spent time together. I'm chalking the night up as a win."

Chapter Two

- Dreamy eyes and eggplant thighs! -

"Bailey, give it a rest. All that barking is going to strain your vocal chords." Elaina ran her fingers through the Pomsky's downy fur.

"We couldn't be that lucky." Steph gave the tiny pooch the stink-eye and tossed her the bright orange knotted chew rope. "Quiet down or you're getting banned to the sunroom for the rest of the day."

Bailey cowered at Elaina's feet as though she understood the threat.

"What's your deal, sweet dog?" Elaina asked.

Steph scoffed. "She's a dog. Sweet? Not so much."

Bailey sought refuge between Elaina's shoes and peeked up at Steph.

"She totally comprehends what you're saying."

"She totally comprehends my tone." Steph shook a finger at the furry dog. "How can such a small thing yap so loudly?"

Grace plodded down the stairs with an unsavory

expression from having been awakened by non-stop barking. "I despise you, Arden Wellby Samuels." She drew her face into a tight frown. "I know he's sitting at his breakfast table, laughing and patting himself on the back for illicit plans well executed. 'Come and get this dog or I'm going to take her to the shelter.' The barracuda bared his teeth and you swooped in to save the day."

"I didn't swoop."

"Oh you swooped all right. You're a swooper."

Bailey stopped barking and cocked his head at Grace.

Elaina stroked Bailey's ears. "She thinks you dissed me."

Stony barreled into the living room, side-swiping the edge of the coffee table and spilling Steph's cup of hot chocolate.

"These animals are driving me insane!" Steph sopped up the chocolate with her napkin. "We have a big dog who thinks he's as light on his feet as a tiny dog and a tiny dog who thinks she has the influence of a big dog."

A creaking noise made their gazes jet to Tawny's bedroom door.

Dressed in red plaid pajama pants, a frayed 'Dogs Rule' t-shirt, fuzzy pea-green Grinch slippers, and her hair matted on one side of her head, Tawny ventured out of her room for the first time since returning home from the hospital.

Grace teased her straight away. "You're alive!"

"I haven't had coffee in three days, so watch it, Ms. Cordray." Tawny planted a kiss on Stony's head and pushed him out of the way to get to the kitchen.

"Ms. Cordray," Grace mocked with a laugh. Bailey barked like a mad dog. And Stony sang harmony with a yowl.

"Life at the Four Sassy Chicks Bed and Breakfast is back to normal."

The weather reared up in disagreement with Elaina. A gust of wind kicked up so hard it rattled the large picture window. Heavy raindrops pelted the glass like they were trying to make their way inside.

"I spoke too soon. Last week, it snowed. Yesterday, the sun was so blinding spectacular, the birds took off their winter coats to frolic in the front yard. Today, Mother Nature is sassier than the four of us put together." Elaina loosened Bailey's collar one notch.

"Birds don't wear coats."

"It's called imagery, Grace." Steph slurped the remainder of her drink and licked the chocolate mustache from her upper lip.

Elaina hopped up from the couch, donned a waterproof parka, and hooked leashes to the two rambunctious dogs. "Despite the rain, it's time to stretch our legs. Come on, Stone-man and Bailey-girl."

Steph sighed. "Bless you, Elaina. I need a few minutes of peace and quiet."

"Let me know if you see any birds wearing coats."

Steph inclined her head toward Grace. "Take her with you."

"I only have two leashes." Elaina bared her teeth in an ornery grin.

"You're a riot."

"I know, right?" To avoid taking the pooches through the kitchen to get outside, Elaina opened the front door and flinched back in surprise.

"Sorry, ma'am, I didn't mean to scare you. I was about to ring the doorbell."

Stony and Bailey tried to crowd in front of Elaina to check out their visitor. She had to use her thigh to hold them back.

Bailey went nuts at being restrained. She barked, turned in a circle, barked some more and twisted the leash until she could no longer move.

Elaina looked over her shoulder. "A little help?"

Steph snapped up Bailey and unwound the leash. Grace tugged Stony to the middle of the room.

Elaina motioned for the dripping-wet man to come in. "It's good to see you again."

"At least this time my face isn't puffy, and I can do more than cough. One minute my friends and I were discussing politics, the next I was wheeled out on a gurney."

"I have an adverse reaction when the conversation turns to politics too."

It took the span of a few seconds for Elaina's wacky humor to register with Kace. "Good one." Good one." He took a white envelope from the inside pocket of his coat and moved so he could look past her. "Is Tawny around?"

Elaina called out to Tawny.

Tawny didn't make an appearance.

"Tawny, you have a guest," she reiterated.

Tawny lazily stuck her head out of the kitchen. Her eyes rounded with surprise when recognized the man she'd aided in the restaurant. "Kace?" Suddenly energized, she trekked across the living room.

Droplets of rain fell from Kace's hair, half saturating the envelope in his hand. "I stopped by to thank you."

Tawny seemed mesmerized by his hair. She tried to smooth hers into looking a little less messy.

Kace lowered his gaze to her feet. "Nice slippers."

"I, uh, please excuse my appearance." She scuffed the end of her slipper back and forth over the floor.

"After you were taken to the hospital, Tawny made a trip there too," Elaina explained.

"Oh no! What happened?" Kace impulsively placed a hand on Tawny's arm. Stony emitted a low growl. Kace withdrew his hand.

"And we're walking." Elaina led both dogs out the door.

* * *

Kicking off her waterlogged sneakers in the breezeway, Elaina traipsed into the kitchen.

"That parka did little to keep the rain off you." Steph tossed her a dry dish towel.

"Sideways rain isn't as much fun as it sounds. I'm literally soaked to the skin."

"How'd the dogs like it?"

"Stony was in his element. He jumped and splashed in the puddles. Bailey was overwhelmed. I left them in the garage for the time being." Elaina blotted rain from her face.

Yips and barks resonated through the walls.

"They're in need of a hot bath as much as I am." A trickle of water ran down Elaina's arm and onto the floor.

Steph ripped off several paper towels from the roll. "Here you go."

Elaina sopped up the puddle and asked how things had gone with Kace and Nightingale.

"I tried to spy. They got wise to me and moved to the sunroom."

"Interesting."

"My thoughts exactly." Steph hacked off the end of an eggplant. "Kace is better looking than I remember."

"We were too concerned with his well-being to notice anything else." Thin streams of rainwater continued to trail down Elaina's forehead and nose.

"He has the dreamiest blue eyes."

Elaina put a finger across her lips. "Shh. Here comes Nick. I'm fairly certain he wouldn't want his best gal talking about another guy's eyes."

"I'm just stating a fact."

"A fact you need to keep between us."

"The day I have to watch what I say, is the day I..." Steph bit down on her bottom lip when Nick's essence filled the room.

"Good morning, ladies."

"Good morning, handsome."

"It is a good morning, despite all the rain." Elaina blotted her face again and toed off her wet shoes.

"Any morning I wake up and the ground isn't covered with snow, it's a great day." Nicholas wrapped Steph in a hug and peered over her shoulder. "Look at the size of that eggplant. What are you making?"

"Lasagna."

Nick released Steph and studied the purple vegetable. "My mom tried to disguise eggplant a thousand different ways and I still couldn't eat it."

"Trust me. You'll love this."

"I doubt it."

Elaina gave Nick's shoulder a small whap. "She can make anything taste good."

Steph's mouth split into an ear to ear grin. "Yeah, what she said. Besides, Nicholas Augustine the first, we're not only getting in shape on the outside, but also on the inside. A few meatless dishes won't kill us."

Nick stood his ground. "Zucchini lasagna I can do. Eggplant isn't going to happen."

Elaina jumped into the fray. "Did you know Kace has dreamy eyes?"

Nick gave Elaina a confused look. "Who's Kace?"

"The guy Tawny saved."

"Oh-kay. I'm not getting the connection between his eyes and eggplant lasagna?"

"I'm sure if we invite dreamy-eyes to stay for Steph's lasagna he would," Elaina teased.

"Did you just put the smack-down on me?"

Elaina showed the muscles in her arm. "Why yes, I think I did."

Nick chuckled and placed his hands on Steph's hips.

"Honey, do you think Kace's eyes are dreamy?"

Steph crossed her fingers, but made sure Nick saw them. "No."

Nick jokingly narrowed his eyes. "I'll eat your stinking lasagna."

Elaina and Steph knuckle-bumped.

"Speaking of stinking, if I don't get those pooches in the shower, they're going to smell like a pair of sweaty gym shoes."

Grace stepped into the kitchen to see what was going on; in her hands, a stack of freshly laundered bath towels. "Is the wet-look the current thing?"

"Getting caught in a torrential downpour is the current thing. So is eggplant lasagna."

"Sounds like a dish I want to avoid."

Nick put his hand up for Grace to give him a high-five. Grace couldn't free her hands and stuck out her elbow for him to smack instead.

Elaina made up a song for Nick. "Ohh, ohh, dreamy eyes. Eggplant lasagna won't hurt my thighs."

Nick rolled his eyes. "Women. You can't live with them and you can't... Wait. You can live with them." He nuzzled Steph's neck. "Let me know when the lasagna is ready." He walked past Elaina and warned that he was watching her by pointing two fingers at his eyes and then at hers.

"I'm watching you too, Nick."

Grace's gaze danced from Nick to Elaina to Steph. "Wanna catch me up?"

* * *

"It's been great talking to you, too." Tawny waved goodbye to Kace. She turned to find Elaina, Steph, and Grace standing shoulder to shoulder, waiting to get the low-down.

"Spill," Steph demanded.

"He seemed taller in the restaurant."

Steph wasn't satisfied. "That's all you've got to say?"

"Yes."

Elaina, Grace, and Steph exchanged curious looks.

Grace asked the question on all three of their minds. "Was there a spark?"

"He gave me a gift membership to the botanical gardens in Boothbay."

Elaina took the membership certificate from Tawny and checked it out. "He's an eyeful and also practical."

"I'm sure his wife also thinks so." Tawny twisted her mouth in contemplation. "It's just my luck. He's married and a lawyer. The entire time we talked, I got stabbing flashbacks of my divorce attorney who basically helped Grady get everything but the kitchen sink. Wait. He got the sink."

"Not all lawyers are the same."

"Mine was cunningly inept. Truth be told, he and Grady were in cahoots." Sarcasm oozed from Tawny. "It's a good thing Kace is taken. His eyes would be enough to make me forget I hold the record when it comes to picking the wrong guy."

"No you don't have the record. I'm the world's worst

man picker." In the span of a heartbeat, Steph changed her tune. "At least I used to be. Nick's terrific, even if he isn't a fan of eggplant."

"I'm happy for you, Steph. Really. My track record, on the other hand, has gotten worse. I'm not depressed or complaining, just stating a fact."

Grace looped an arm through Tawny's and led them to the book nook where they'd placed a computer for their guests to use. "You should fill out an online dating profile. That way you can sort through the nincompoops and find your hunk."

"I don't think so." She tried to get up and Grace pushed her back down. "Seriously, I'm not in the market for male attention at this time; even if I were, it wouldn't go down this way. I prefer to find men the old fashioned way." She inhaled and exhaled dramatically. "I want the body-tingling sensation of attraction the moment I lay eyes on someone."

"You can still have all that on your first date," Grace stated like she was a dating expert.

"It's not the same as spontaneous fire."

Grace mimicked banging her head. "Head desk."

Elaina smoothed a hand over Tawny's shoulders. "Is that how it was with you and Grady? Did things ignite between you right away?"

The question caught Tawny by surprise. Her eyes flared open and she tipped her head to the side as though reliving the memory. "As much as I hate to admit it, that's exactly how it happened."

Elaina's thoughts rushed to Jess Blakefield. They'd had

some powerful chemistry too. His kisses had scrambled her brain, and she'd been struggling to get back on track. Jess had set her body and soul on fire and then moved to Virginia. He said the relocation would be temporary. Elaina was finding that the longer he was gone, the more it felt permanent. She gave herself an internal shake to stop thinking about him. "You could feel that kind of fire again, Tawn', but it would involve putting yourself out there."

"Online pursuance is a huge no. What other venues are there? Please don't mention the grocery or church."

"There's always the gas station." Elaina anticipated a frown, and Tawny didn't let her down.

"Your ways to meet men are freaking strange."

Wit was not a gift Elaina didn't claim to possess. But that didn't stop her from embracing the silly. "You could troll Laundromats."

Grace and Steph split a gut laughing.

Tawny grimaced.

Steph tried a different tactic. "There are a range of choices that don't involve Laundromats or gas stations. I read online... Stop sneering and hear me out. I read online that there are singles groups you can join. For a small fee, you can attend special functions: meetups, karaoke and movie nights, dances, and more. If that doesn't ring your chimes, there are plenty of singles bars to explore. I suggest going another route though." Steph winked at Elaina. "She's going to hate me for this, but if she finds someone who makes her body tingle she'll un-hate me."

Tawny arched an eyebrow as high as it would go. "What's the suggestion?"

Steph clicked her pearly whites together. "Speed-dating."

"Let the hating begin."

"You know you love me. The way I see it, you have two choices: whine every day until the rest of us buy high-quality earplugs to block you out, or you can try one of the aforementioned ideas and see if it pans out."

"Again, I'm not in the market for a companion. But humor me. How does one speed-date?"

"The rules are simple. You'll be given a card to mark down men you're interested in during the session. You'll get four minutes of conversation with each guy. A bell will ring, signaling the guy to move to the next woman for another round of four minutes. At the end of the gathering, you hand in your card. The organizers will provide you with contact information for those who didn't turn you off."

"Have you speed-dated?"

A sheepish look crossed Steph's expression. "Right after Corbett kicked me to the curb, I tried it."

"Whaaaat?" Grace clutched Steph's arm and gave it a shake. "Why are we just now hearing about this?"

"Because it was a disaster."

"But it's okay for me to try? I don't think so, crazy lady."

Steph made mean eyes at Tawny. "Let me finish. As I was saying, it was a disaster...because of me. The moment the first round began, I got tongue-tied and couldn't form a coherent sentence." She sighed. "In the second round, the contents of my stomach inched up and I thought I was going to hurl."

"When you're trying to sell someone an idea, you don't mention barfing, Steph."

"I'm confident you won't barf, Tawny. Elaina you should do it with her."

Elaina put a finger in her mouth and pretended to gag.

Chapter Three

- Some days you have to switch things up! -

The next three weeks were a happy blur of activity, thanks to an influx of guests who made reservations at the last minute. Thoughts of speed-dating, clubbing, and visiting gas stations to find men were put on hold. Word about the Four Sassy Chicks Bed and Breakfast had spread around the country, and folks came from as far away as Texas, Arkansas, and Utah.

Elaina was up to her elbows in laundry, bathroom detail, making breakfasts, and taking care of Stony and Bailey. In the midst of all that busyness, Grace and Philip started renovating their Victorian home across the street. Steph and Nick had to put in extra hours at the restaurant because two of their hardworking employees had fallen for each other, eloped, and moved to Montana. Tawny's current gig at the hospital involved twelve-hour stints in the emergency room. She came home dog-tired, with unbelievable stories. While she wouldn't name names, she'd share the wild bustle that took place during her shift and then camp out in her bedroom to recover so she could start all over again in another twelve hours.

Life was chaotic and incredible at the same time.

This particular morning was a doozy. Elaina was juggling breakfast and accommodating their guests, while Tawny tried to keep Bailey from chewing things; most especially the wooden leg of their purple Gothic beast of a loveseat. Ten minutes behind schedule, Tawny didn't have time to actually correct or punish Bailey so she turned the discipline over to Elaina.

Wiping sweat from above her brow, Elaina placed scrambled eggs in a chafing dish.

One of the guests came up behind Elaina, scaring the bejesus out of her. "Ma'am, I'm not keen on scrambled. Could I get a couple of eggs over easy?"

Guests had filled out their breakfast preferences on a slip the night before. This particular gentleman hadn't marked anything other than oatmeal.

Elaina reminded herself that it would only be hectic for a while and to put a smile in place. "I'd be happy to make you any kind of eggs you want."

Another guest decided to change his order. "I'd like mine over easy too."

A third guest followed suit.

Elaina polled the others and received similar requests. "I'm on it." While she wasn't in favor of diverting from the menu, she knew happy guests were good for business.

"Any chance a guy could get some sausage gravy and biscuits?"

"I can make it happen, although it might take fifteen

to twenty minutes." Thank goodness Steph had made and frozen several packages of sausage gravy. Elaina would have to rely on store-bought biscuits though. But hey, they were quick and tasted ten times better than the ones she made. Steph, on the other hand, could make biscuits from scratch without following a recipe and they practically melted in your mouth. Since Steph was unavailable, the Pillsbury doughboy would be put to good use.

"You're the best," the man said. "I've never stayed in a more comfortable, homey bed and breakfast."

"Thank you. That's good to know."

The man's wife knocked his arm with her elbow. "This is our first bed and breakfast."

A huge grin splashed into the man's face. "Busted."

"It's all good. Eggs over easy, sausage gravy and biscuits are coming right up."

"Do you have tomato juice," the same man asked. "And maybe some vodka, horseradish, Tabasco sauce, ice cubes, lemon juice, and celery? Oh, and a pinch of salt."

"Ahh. You'd like a Bloody Mary with your breakfast." Elaina chuckled. A Blood Mary actually sounded good. Without looking in the liquor cabinet, she knew there was just a smidgen of vodka left in the bottle, barely enough for a glass, certainly not enough for a pitcher. "No can do. I'll put vodka at the top of my shopping list. In the meantime, we could make virgin Bloody Marys."

He wasn't sold on the idea. "What's the point?"

"Tomatoey goodness without the kick."

"I'd rather have the kick, but I'll settle for tomatoey goodness."

His wife cut him with an annoyed look.

Twenty minutes later, with breakfast food and drinks – sans vodka, those at the table discussed how they'd spend the day. One of the older couples planned to take a ferry over to Peaks Island. A younger couple couldn't wait to check out the microbreweries in the area. The youngest couple made googly eyes at each other and didn't offer their plans.

The guy who'd asked for over-easy eggs and vodka, insisted Elaina join them at the table.

"I guess I can sit for a few minutes." She poured a cup of coffee, took a seat, and smiled at the couple going to Peaks Island. "Did you know there are 4600 islands off the coast of Maine? There are some islands inland as well."

The older couple unfolded a pamphlet listing the islands with ferry service to and from Portland. They asked a slew of questions. Elaina could only answer a few.

"We've been in Maine since November, so we haven't had much opportunity to get out and discover all that this awesome state has to offer."

The younger couple perked up when someone mentioned there was a cryptozoology museum in Portland dedicated to the study of hidden or unknown creatures like Big Foot, Yetis, and Lake Monsters. All eyes swung to Elaina.

"It's located at Thompson's Point and close to the

Portland Transportation Center." Everyone continued looking attentively at Elaina, expecting her to delve deeper into the subject. If guests wanted to glean advice, she'd have to learn more about the city she lived in and actually make time to visit the attractions. "I hear they have one-of-a-kind zoological specimens." Elaina sipped her coffee. Over the rim of the cup, she smiled. "That's all I've got."

Bailey yipped until everyone paid attention.

Elaina looked over the half-doors that kept the tiny dog from the kitchen and dining area. Bailey was attacking the purple Gothic monstrosity again like it was a bone. "Not today, sweet pooch. Not today." Instead of letting the ball of fluff have her way with the furniture, Elaina relocated her to the basement where a soft cushy bed lay in a wire kennel. "Sorry, Bailey-girl, you get to take a nap. I could use a timeout too."

* * *

"Did Portland have a marathon I didn't know about? And did you take part?"

Elaina gave Tawny a lopsided grin. She was well aware of her ragamuffin appearance, yet she was too bushed to care. Haphazard strands of hair framed her face in damp wisps and perspiration soaked the neckline of the ratty t-shirt she'd put on after returning home from transporting all guests to the airport. "I started spring cleaning."

"We straighten and sanitize the guest rooms, and

the main rooms, the moment the guests leave. Any and all dog hair is taken care of practically before it hits the floor. Essentially, this house is sterile, yet you wipe down things that aren't dirty. Now you're spring cleaning." Tawny tapped her chin with her finger. "I think your cleanliness obsession has more to do with wanting a distraction from the hamsters spinning on the wheel in your head."

"You're reading too much into it." Elaina returned the bottle of spray cleaner to the utility closet.

"Am I?" Tawny studied her from where she was propped against the kitchen counter. "You're staying busy to keep your mind off Jess."

"You are so wrong."

"I am so right and you know it."

Elaina let her shoulders fall. "I'm waiting around for someone who won't return. Before he left for Virginia the second time, I told Jess I loved him. I said, 'I thought you should know.' What did he say back? Not 'I love you too.' He said, 'You should know there are fault lines in Maine.'"

"He's attracted to you. That much is obvious. The state of his heart, however, remains a mystery. Guys are wired differently. Most aren't as open about their feelings as we'd like them to be. It becomes a freaking guessing game with them."

"My dad always told my mom that he loved her."

"But you weren't privy to how things were in their early days. I'd bet money your mom played the guessing game too."

Elaina chuckled. "I can't picture them holding anything back. They were so much in love and so in synch."

"You got to see them at their best." Tawny filled a glass with water and chugged half of it in one swallow. "Has Jess texted you lately?"

"I haven't heard from him in weeks."

"Have you sent him messages?"

"Every day."

Tawny's eyes practically bugged out of their sockets. "What? No! That's not how to do it."

"Isn't communication the key to a good relationship?"

"It definitely is when the messages go back and forth. You send one, he sends one back. When the other person resists...."

Hearing Tawny break it down for her, reminded Elaina of what she already knew. "I've been acting like a needy puppy."

"Yes you have. Now snap out of it. You told Jess how you feel. This is cliché, but the ball is in his court. If he volley's it back, he wants to keep you in his life. If he doesn't, then you have to accept that he's keeping the damn ball and you need to move on."

Elaina felt sick to her stomach. She'd become weird and clingy. "I'm usually not this pathetic."

"It happens to the best of us. You have a good head on your shoulders, yet you're not immune to occasionally screwing up. My best advice at this moment is to restore your dignity by NOT sending him anything until he reciprocates."

"I've been telling myself I don't want to be in a special relationship. Deep down it isn't true. I miss holding hands and being kissed."

"Do you miss sex?"

Elaina pressed her lips together to keep from saying yes.

Tawny laughed. "Of course you do. You're human."

"I've been trying to force Jess to fulfill my desires."

"Well, it's time to back off. Do something different. I'm not sure what it might be, but change things up until you're happy." Tawny started to open the refrigerator and stopped to read the grocery list attached to the door with a magnet. "Eggs, milk, bread, cantaloupe, vodka." She turned with a smirk. "Vodka?"

* * *

"These are so good." Steph stirred her Bloody Mary with the stalk of celery and took another taste. "Why are we wasting time with wine when we can be drinking these bad boys?"

Grace said that calling them the No Sweat Pants Allowed – Bloody Mary Club was just plain weird. It makes us sound like serial killers or that our menses have synched."

Steph wagged a finger. "Taboo subject."

"Menses?" Grace laughed and teetered into Elaina's shoulder. "I may have had too many glasses of tomato juice."

"Noooo, you had too many ounces of vodka." Tawny

lifted Grace's glass to the light. "I see more vodka than tomato juice. Why?"

"I'm not a mixologist. I don't know the ratio of vodka to tomato juice."

Tawny fanned the recipe card Steph had made. "It's right here in black and white. A real answer, please."

Grace pulled at her bottom lip with her teeth. "Sometimes a girl needs more vodka than tomato juice to cope with a bossy boyfriend."

"Now we're getting somewhere."

Elaina sat Grace up straight. "Is Philip being a pain?"

"Understatement. He's been a bossy crab for a couple weeks."

"Want me to take him out?" Tawny offered with a goofy grin.

Grace appeared to mull over the offer. "No, Tawn'. Not yet anyway. I gave him an ultimatum – sweeten up or it's hasta la vista, baby."

Tawny raised her eyebrows. "No way."

"Way."

"Grace, you little fireball."

"I don't have to settle for cranky. Not when there are a ton of lovable guys out there."

Tawny scoffed. "And where exactly would they be located?"

"You want me to name a place?"

"Yes. Name a place."

"Providence, Rhode Island."

Everyone laughed, including Grace.

"That brain of yours amazes me, Cordray." Elaina

imbibed in another sip of Bloody Mary. "Providence may have a ton of available, lovable men, but I think we can find you one that isn't three hours away."

"I don't wish to replace Philip. I'm just venting."

Steph munched on the celery from her drink. While she chewed, you could see her cogs turning. "You issued him an ultimatum. Be careful there, Grace. Men tend to take what we say at face value."

"I know they do." Grace pinched her fingers together to show an inch in length. "I told him to sweeten up or else, and I meant it this much. For the time being, Philip and I are still a couple. Enough about us. Steph you have Nicholas. Tawny and Elaina are menless. We have to hook them up."

"Is menless a real word?"

"Yes."

"I don't think it is." Elaina tapped an app on her phone.

"It's not a real word, okay? Stop messing with your phone. You and Tawny are going to fill out online dating profiles right now." Regardless of Elaina's immediate objection, Grace tugged her out of the chair and gripped her wrist. "To the computer we go."

Elaina tried to pry Grace's fingers loose. The effort was in vain. Grace had a grip like a vise.

"Stop squawking. Start typing."

Tawny elbowed Elaina, "And she thinks Philip is bossy."

They traded amused looks.

Tawny said with more conviction than needed, that

she wasn't chancing an online rejection. "The ones I get in person are bad enough."

Grace finally let go of Elaina. "Need I remind you that in some cases you've been the rejector?"

Tawny pointed to the floor with her thumbs. "Nevertheless, two thumbs-down to this mode of hooking up."

Elaina nodded in agreement. "I'm old-school too. There isn't enough alcohol in Maine…or Rhode Island… to make me want to find a virtual man."

Tawny laughed like a maniac. She snorted, held her stomach, and laughed some more.

Steph looked bewildered and asked if she'd missed something.

"You did not." A sheepish grin spread across Tawny's face.

"Then what?"

"I cannot lie to my wine club ladies."

Steph pinged her glass with a flick to remind Tawny they weren't drinking wine.

"Nor can I fib to my Bloody Mary ladies. Today," Tawny paused, "on my lunch break I filled out a profile."

Elaina's mouth fell open. "You just said you didn't want to risk rejection."

"I don't want to be rejected. That much is true." Tawny pushed Elaina down into the computer chair. "I put myself out there. Now it's your turn."

"You gave into peer pressure, obviously. That's your deal, not mine."

"Listen you blonde-haired goat, you said you missed holding hands and kissing."

Elaina was ticked in an instant. "I told you that in confidence."

Tawny pulled the neckline of her shirt down to expose the fairly new tattoo she'd gotten that read, One of Four Sassy Chicks. "Remember this? We all have one." Then she lifted her ankle to reveal the infinity tattoo that represented their eternal friendship. "We each have one of these too. We're a foursome of forever. What you say to me, you say to the others."

"If I tell you to kiss my butt, I'm also telling the others to do the same?"

"Now you're getting it."

Elaina put as much dry sarcasm into her reply as she could drum up. "I don't want to do this."

"I'll fill one out for you. The male population will soon know you're into whips and chains, and that you enjoy being drizzled with maple syrup."

Elaina backhanded Tawny. "You're grossing me out."

Tawny gestured to the computer. "Then get those fingers dancing across the keyboard."

* * *

Steph slung her purse on her shoulder and handed Elaina the reservation ledger. "I took a reservation earlier for the end of May. A couple from Wyoming will be coming with their dog Reggie."

"Awesome."

"I'm headed to the restaurant again. Nick got a call an hour ago that another waitress quit." She groaned. "He left right away to find out what's going on with his help. Employees seem to be jumping ship just when things are getting super busy. Nick's getting nervous."

"Sorry to hear that. Do what you can to keep him calm."

Someone pressed the doorbell six times in a row.

"I've got to go." Steph gave Elaina a quick hug and ducked out the back door.

Elaina rushed to find out who continued to incessantly ring the bell.

Propped up by canes, an old couple stood smiling on the porch. At their feet lay an overnight bag.

"Hello. Welcome to the Four Sassy Chicks Bed and Breakfast. How can I help you?"

The tiny woman teetered sideways into the man. "We're Ruth and Gordie from Bangor."

"Nice to meet you, Ruth and Gordie."

"Likewise." Ruth peered around Elaina. "Do you have a vacancy?"

The sign outside said as much, but sometimes people used it as a lead-in.

"We do. Please come in." Due to their ages, which Elaina estimated to be early to mid-eighties, it took them a while to get inside. She helped with their bag. "I need some information from you, and then I'll show you around."

"Oh, hon, you don't have to show us around. Just show us to our room." Ruth looked adoringly at her husband.

They followed Elaina to the dining table.

"All right, folks, have a seat." Again, it took monumental effort for them to get into chairs. "I'm Elaina – one of the four sassy chicks. The others are Tawny, Steph, and Grace. You'll meet them later in the day."

Ruth and Gordie sat quietly.

"The first thing I have to ask is if you have any special dietary needs."

Ruth made eyes at her husband. "The only dietary need I have is more of Gordie."

Elaina didn't know what to make of the comment. "Aww, how sweet." Returning to the paperwork, she informed them they could pay with a credit card and she had to see their driver's licenses.

"Young lady, Ruth and I are eighty-four years old and refuse to get a credit card. People have had their identities stolen as a result of those blasted things."

Ruth snuggled against him. "We had our car stolen once from the parking lot of a motel. It was my fault, really. Gordie said he didn't want to stay there, I insisted. I should've listened to him. That was twenty years ago, when we were living fast and loose."

In their sixties they lived fast and loose? Elaina reminded herself not to judge.

Ruth winked at Gordie. "Remember those days, hon?"

Gordie's chuckle was raspy. "I've forgotten a lot of things, but there's no way I can forget your wild ways. They're forever cemented in my brain, doll." He gave her a slow-motion peck on the mouth.

Elaina hated to crimp all that gushy love stuff, but she had towels to fold and a kitchen floor to mop. "In lieu of a credit card, would it offend you if I asked for payment up front?"

"Not at all, Eloise," Gordie stated.

Ruth patted his wrinkled hand. "It's Elaina, not Eloise."

"Oh. Sorry, miss."

"No worries. How long do you folks plan to stay?"

Ruth handled the question. "At our age, we only book one day at a time." She opened her large black purse and took out a roll of cash secured with a rubber band. Slapping five bills on the table, she said, "That should cover it."

"Ruth, that's too much."

A strange smile curved the frail woman's mouth. "Consider it a security deposit in case anything gets damaged."

"I doubt anything will get damaged." Elaina almost said that she bumped into things all the time. She played the words in her head first and decided she'd come off as patronizing. Instead, she smiled and repeated her wish to see their driver's licenses.

Gordie joined the conversation again. "Eloise, we haven't had driver's licenses since we failed the eye test."

Elaina wouldn't correct him about her name; Ruth had already done it once. If he wanted to call her Eloise, so be it. She was curious about their lack of driver's licenses since there was an older model Plymouth sitting in front of the house. Surely Gordie was messing with her. In case he wasn't, Elaina produced some truth. "For liability reasons, our insurance carrier dictates that we identify our guests."

Ruth and Gordie looked at each other with soulful eyes. Ruth went so far as to whimper. "We won't cause you any trouble, I promise. We're just a couple of old lovebirds who still have some wanderlust in us." She hacked like she was trying to cough up a lung. "We can only stare at the same old walls for so long, and then we take an excursion."

Elaina silently questioned whether they'd escaped from a nursing home or assisted living facility. "Did you take Route 1 down? Or brave the turnpike?"

"Turnpike," Gordie said without hesitation. "People gawk too much on Route 1 and they impede my driving."

Apparently your vision impedes your driving too.

"I like to put the pedal to the metal and get us to our destination while we're still breathing." Gordie cracked up laughing and sent himself into a wheezing fit.

"Are you okay?"

He couldn't stop wheezing long enough to respond.

Elaina felt for her phone in the back pocket of her jeans in case she needed to call for help. "Is he okay, Ruth?"

"He's fine. He gets to laughing and his lungs can't keep up."

And just like that, he was back to normal.

No credit cards. No driver's licenses. Now what? "Do you have any form of identification?"

"I'm sorry we don't."

Crap. Double crap. It was time to pull a rabbit out of her hat. "I don't mean to nag, really, I don't. But in order to stay here, you'll have to provide emergency contact information."

Sparse, silvery eyebrows bumped together. "9-1-1 is the only emergency contact number I know."

"I meant the name and phone number of a relative."

"Ohhhh." Gordie looked at Ruth. "I guess we won't be staying here."

They started to get up.

"I promise I won't nark you out to that person. It's not my place to do so. The only way I'd use the phone number is if a serious medical issue arose." Elaina raised her palm like she was swearing an oath.

"What do you think, Ruth?"

Ruth yawned. "We're staying. I need a nap."

And I need a glass of vodka with a splash of tomato juice.

Chapter Four

~ Unusual guests and goat cheese! ~

Elaina huddled Tawny, Steph, and Grace together, and spoke as quietly as possible. Gordie and Ruth couldn't see three feet in front of them; nothing said they didn't have the exceptional hearing of bats. "I kid you not. They're eighty-four, have no credit cards or any form of ID, including no driver's licenses. They drove here from Bangor on I-95."

A series of repetitive thuds coming from Gordie and Ruth's room put them on high alert.

Grace's light blue eyes darkened with concern. "I hope they're not trying to signal us for help. Maybe we should have call-buttons installed in each room."

Tawny mocked with a head tilt. "We're not having call-buttons installed and I doubt they're trying to signal us. They're probably propped up against the headboard watching TV and every time they shift around the wood hits the wall."

"It's a heavy four-post bed. The headboard shouldn't

hit the wall when they move to get comfortable."

Steph tiptoed to their door and cupped her ear against the wood. She shook her head and crept back to the kitchen. "Their TV isn't on and I swear I heard moaning."

Elaina was getting more concerned by the second. "What do we do?"

"We wait," Tawny stated matter-of-factly.

"For the stench of decomposing bodies?"

Tawny rolled her eyes at Steph. "Get real."

"Steph might be on to something. How do I word this delicately?"

"To heck with being delicate, just say it," Tawny urged.

Elaina shared the sad reality. "Time isn't something that Gordie and Ruth have on their side."

"Did they come here to...?" Grace splayed a hand across her face. "Ugh. I can't even."

"I'm sure their plan wasn't to check in and extinguish their...lights. It could be a matter of all that living fast and loose catching up with them."

Tawny's brows twitched with confusion. "Say again?""You heard me."

"Geez. Leave you in charge for a week and you interrogate our customers about their past. Are you that bored?" Tawny's mouth split into an ornery grin.

Elaina gave her a playful shove. "They volunteered the information."

"Sure they did."

"The three of you can stand there and wait for whatever might or might not be happening. I'm going upstairs to shower." Grace pulled at the t-shirt with splotches of beige paint on the front. "Philip got his way as you can see. I wanted to paint the parlor a deep blue, but noooo, he bought beige."

"Is he still being a grouch?"

"Nope. He's had a magical transformation." Grace started to leave.

"Graaaace, hold up." Steph grabbed the back of Grace's shirt. "You can't dangle a carrot and walk away."

"Unhand me." Grace wrinkled her nose with amusement. "I told him to straighten up or I would check into those dating sites you ladies love."

Elaina bunched her face into a teasing frown. "You're a mean little woman."

"Philip said the same thing."

Grace made it as far as the first step on the staircase.

Gordie and Ruth's door flung open. Gordie stood in the doorway shirtless. Tufts of gray hair went every which way.

"Gordie, these are the other sassy chicks." She introduced Grace as the business manager, Steph as their kitchen goddess, and Tawny as the resident nurse.

"I don't need a nurse, Eloise. I need water. All that 'action' has made me thirsty." He clicked his tongue.

"Eloise?"

"Long story, Tawn'," Elaina whispered out of the side of her mouth and hoped Tawny and the others wouldn't make a huge deal out of his reference to 'action'. "There's a small refrigerator near the desk, Gordie." The amenities were explained when she'd shown them the room. It now appeared that they were more excited to get 'busy' rather than to actually listen. Instinct made her feet move, but Gordie stopped her by jutting out a spindly arm.

"You might not want to come closer. Ruth's too hot to put clothes on or to cover with a blanket. Give her a few minutes."

"Right." Elaina heard Tawny's restrained tee-hee'ing behind her. To keep her own laughter from spilling out, she bit the inside of her cheek and diverted her gaze to Grace, who noiselessly mouthed the word, "Unbelievable."

"On second thought, do you have any energy drinks? The pill's doing what it's supposed to, but I'm drained."

Steph had yet to put two and two together. "Has your sugar level dropped?"

Elaina glanced at Steph. "His sugar's fine."

"Then what?"

Tawny blurted, "Do we really need to spell it out?"

Steph got huffy right away. "No!" Awareness hit her a milli-second later. "Ohhhh."

The nurse in Tawny took over. "I don't want to boss you around, but it isn't wise to combine an energy drink with that particular pill, or any pill for that matter."

"That's what Ruth says."

Elaina could no longer contain her laughter. She giggled until she snorted. "Gordie, you and Ruth are a hoot. I don't think I've ever met anyone quite like you."

"Did you hear that, Ruth? Eloise thinks we're a hoot."

Ruth's reprimand was wobbly and low. "Gordie, get it

together. Her name is Elaina, not Eloise."

Gordie's whiskery face fell. "Sorry, Elaina."

"No worries. Really." She didn't want him to dwell on the mistake, so she changed the subject. "I noticed that you and Ruth skipped dinner."

"We don't know our way around Portland. We thought we'd wait until morning and eat a big breakfast."

Breakfast wasn't for another twelve hours. There's no way Elaina could make them wait that long. They had likely expended their calorie reserves by knocking the headboard against the wall. "Are you interested in leftover meatloaf, cheesy potatoes, and applesauce?"

"Dear girl, you're a godsend."

"She's more motherly than godsend-ish," Tawny teased.

I'm more of a sap than godsend-ish, but hey, I am what I am.

* * *

"This can't be good." Grace parted the sheer curtains to get a better look.

Tawny joined her at the window. "Now what did we do?" She walked to the security alarm on the wall behind the front door. "We haven't set this thing off since the day we arrived."

"Is there a patrolman ready to pounce?"

"There are two ready to pounce."

At Elaina's sharp intake of air, Tawny offered a lengthier explanation. "They don't have their weapons drawn and I'm not seeing a S.W.A.T. insignia on their jackets."

The ring of the doorbell made Grace ask, "Bad news? Good news? Any bets as to which it is?"

Tawny expression was hard to read, but her tone said a lot. "Law enforcement showing up at the door for no obvious reason sends chills up my spine. It's a parent's worst nightmare."

Grace sighed. "Sorry. I never gave that a thought. Although, just because we're miles away from our kids doesn't mean...."

"Don't let your minds jump to the worst case scenario." Elaina opened the door and presented the officers a friendly smile. "Good morning."

The lead officer tipped his hat. "Good morning, ma'am. We hate to bother you, but we took a call from Bangor P.D." He checked the pocket-size notebook in his hand and threw out Ruth and Gordie's names. "Are they currently staying here?"

Elaina tried not to assume the amorous couple had done something illegal on their trip down from Bangor – like rob a bank; especially since they were in possession of a sheaf of cash. It was doubtful they were involved in a heist – doing so would've required quick reflexes, the capacity to run, and great eyesight. They didn't have any of those things. "Yes, sir, they're here." Her gaze traveled to where Ruth and Gordie sat enjoying hash brown casserole, bacon, and blueberries. "Are we in danger?"

The lead officer looked at the second one, as if asking for approval to proceed. He received a nod. "The only dangers Ruth and Gordie present are to themselves. Their son notified Bangor P.D. that his parents were missing. He'd gone to the market and when he returned home they were gone and so was his vehicle."

"Did you ping their cell phones? Is that how you found them?"

"No. They left their phones on the nightstand in their bedroom. This isn't the first time they've driven off to parts unknown. Their son finally had a tracking device installed to low-jack his vehicle. With his mother being severely diabetic, he's frantic. We don't have any choice but to take them into protective custody."

A low whimper escaped from Elaina. "Good thing I made them eat dinner last night."

The cop gave her a questioning look.

"They didn't want to go out to dinner because..." Elaina cut short the reason, stepped out on the porch, and closed the door behind her. "Officers, they haven't caused any problems."

"They broke the law by driving without licenses."

"You didn't actually see them drive."

"We're not going to put them behind bars. However, we are going to make sure they get back to their son safe and sound."

"This may be a strange request, but could I drive them home?"

The officer shook his head. "They're our responsibility."

"What if their son gave his okay?"

"I'd have to clear it with the captain too."

"Would you? Please?"

For her begging, she received a half-smile.

The lead officer asked his partner to go back to the cruiser and make the calls.

"They really are a sweet couple, sir."

"Their son said as much. He also said they're a handful. Taking care of aging parents can be a challenge. A while back he made the tough decision to put them in assisted living. They gave the staff so many headaches that he was urged to find another facility. Instead, he retired so he could take care of them personally."

"Great news. You have permission to take Ruth and Gordie back to Bangor. I'll need you to sign a statement that you'll leave immediately and deliver them to their son." The officer handed Elaina the clipboard.

She skimmed the document. "You hereby agree to transport..." It was a lot of legal jargon that placed the liability on her shoulders. Elaina signed on the dotted line. "Thank you for your compassion, gentlemen."

"Gordie and Ruth know how to manipulate a situation. Be careful, miss."

Elaina watched the patrol car drive away and then stared at the carbon copy of the agreement. "What have you gotten yourself into this time, Samuels?"

Tawny and Grace stood in the foyer waiting for the scoop.

"Road trip."

Grace folded her arms across her chest. "Because?"

"We've never been to Bangor."

* * *

"Being forced to go home sucks." Gordie grumbled from the back seat.

Elaina had hit the child-lock button, so those feisty octogenarians couldn't flee when she stopped for red lights and stop signs – not that they were capable, but she wouldn't put it past them to turn an easy drive into a hair-pulling experience. Tawny followed in Elaina's Escalade, but it wasn't like she could pull over on the freeway and help chase down two elderly escapees. Grace and Steph had made excuses to stay in Portland. Elaina should've insisted they come along. "I understand your feelings." *And you were clearly in the wrong.*

"It's our lives. We should be able to do what we want."

"I agree with you to a point, Ruth, but your life has changed." Elaina wouldn't mention Ruth's illness. It wasn't her place to know about it, or use it in this conversation. "You're older now and your son wants to protect you."

"He can go suck an egg," Ruth screeched defiantly.

Elaina looked in the rearview mirror. "He loves you."

Ruth's eyes misted right away. "He smothers us."

"Have you discussed this with him?"

Ruth's head bobbed up and down. "All the time."

"Do you talk calmly or bust his chops?"

Gordie didn't sugar-coat the truth. "She busts his chops every time."

"Therein lays your problem. Growing up, did he resist things you wanted him to do?"

"Absolutely."

"Did his actions upset you?"

"Of course they did. He was sixteen, we're eighty-four. You're comparing apples to oranges. Our son doesn't respect our wishes, so we take matters into our own hands." Gordie's sigh of frustration was shaky and weak.

Elaina knew which path she had to take with this discussion. "I appreciate your desire to maintain independence and dignity."

"There's a BUT coming, Gordie. I can feel it."

"Ruth, please listen to what I have to say. It's important." Elaina's airway was unexpectedly and nervously obstructed. She coughed twice to get the air in her windpipe moving again. "I lost my parents a few years ago in a fiery crash." She paused to let that sink in; although, it affected her more than she could've anticipated. The memory wracked her body with a powerful tremble. Tears gushed out, stinging her eyes and momentarily blurring her vision. Her legs shook hard. Thank God she'd enabled cruise control.

"We're sorry for your loss, Eloise."

Elaina disregarded Gordie's constant error of her name and inhaled a deep breath in an effort to regain her emotional balance. "I never got to say goodbye to them. Everyone says grief gets easier to manage as time goes on. I'm still waiting for that to happen. I get through most days without breaking down, yet the hurt is still raw. I'd love to sit and have coffee with them; to share my day, and listen to the things that are important to them. I'd love to take them to doctor's appointments and out to dinner at their favorite restaurant. I'd love to see them smile and hear their voices." She brushed at the tears and sniffed hard since she didn't have a tissue handy. "Your son is lucky to still have you in his life and you're blessed to have him as well. Don't waste precious time trying to escape. If you want to travel, stop busting his chops. Ask him nicely to take you where you want to go. I'm sure he's a reasonable guy. Here's the big BUT you were waiting for – BUT you have to exercise some restraint and respect him as much as you want him to respect you. Taking care of you is a gift, BUT sometimes you stretch the limit of that gift by stressing him out. Give the poor guy a break."

Ruth groaned like she was in pain.

"Are you okay, Ruth?"

"All this feelings-crap is making me cranky."

"Could we stop for pie and coffee?" Gordie asked. "She'll sweeten up once she gets a slice of sugar cream and some java."

Elaina had gotten them almost to Bangor and she feared they'd give her the slip if they went into a restaurant. "Coffee we can do. The pie will have to come later, after I safely deliver you." There was no way she'd be responsible for Ruth's uptick in sugar due to pie.

From out of the blue, Gordie said, "You're holding us captive."

"I have a paper from the Portland Police Department that says otherwise."

Ruth asked, "Why did you volunteer to drive us home? We could be serial killers for all you know."

Elaina smiled straight away. "Are you a serial killer?"

"No."

"Knew it," Elaina spouted. "You're funny, lovable people that I've had the pleasure to meet."

"We aren't happy that you're aiding and abetting the cops, but we're happy to have landed in your lap." Gordie patted Elaina's shoulder. "You're a good gal." He blinked at her in the rearview mirror. "Is there a guy in the picture?"

"Sadly, no."

"Why not?"

"I ask myself that question all the time."

"Do you have trouble in the sack?"

Elaina was only mildly jarred by the question. Older people sometimes lost their filters; Gordie and Ruth definitely had lost theirs. "Let's just say the only heat in my life comes when I eat jalapenos."

* * *

Tawny gave Elaina the side-eye. "You bawled like a freaking baby."

"How could I NOT bawl? How could YOU not bawl? It was an emotional reunion. Their son cried so hard when we pulled into the driveway. He was a mess. I lost it when he wrapped his arms around his mom and dad like he'd never let them go."

"We should've left right away, but no, you had to hang around and plead their case for them."

"I couldn't just drop and run. He had to know his parents' side of the story."

"You don't have to take on everyone's problems."

"That's not what I do." At Tawny's pointed look, Elaina shrugged. "Okay, maybe I do."

Tawny turned left off Stillwater Avenue onto Broadway Street. "Misfits find their way to you. I did. Grace did. So did Steph."

"I'm a misfit too, and I'd kill for a glass of wine right now."

Tawny clicked her tongue. "You and I are so on the same page. While you were busy wa-wa'ing over Gordie and Ruth, I asked Siri about wineries in the area. I found one on Hammond Street with a ton of great reviews. Not only do they have great wine, goat cheese, and ambiance, but also a slew of appetizers to choose from."

Elaina mischievously raised and lowered her eyebrows. "You had me at goat cheese."

"Have you ever tasted goat cheese?"

"I have not," Elaina admitted.

"Well then, you're in for a real treat."

At Broadway and Hammond, Tawny checked the navigation screen and turned left.

"Why am I in for a treat?"

Tawny explained that goat cheese had a different taste. "It's kind of tart and earthy."

"By earthy, do you mean dirt?"

"Noooo."

"You have no idea what it means. You read the description from the business' website, didn't you?"

Tawny beamed a teasing look of guilt.

"As a selling point, I guess it's better to say the cheese tastes earthy, rather than muddy."

"We definitely have to give it a try."

Elaina shifted around in the passenger seat. "What's your schedule like for the next couple of days?"

"I don't work until the weekend. Why?"

"Let's not go back to Portland tonight."

"Gordie and Ruth sell you on the exhilaration of escape?"

"Sort of."

Tawny drummed the steering wheel. "It's funny how things work out. You got through to them, and they got through to you. I should send them a thank-you card."

"You should. Now get me to wine, STAT."

The winery was located just a few blocks from Gordie and Ruth's home. In less than ten minutes, they were seated at a table near the window with glasses of blackberry Merlot.

The lone employee at the winery brought a plate loaded with crackers and a small ball of cheese in the center. "Where are you gals from?"

Tawny sat up straighter, which made her bountiful chest take center stage. It was something Elaina noticed Tawny did when a member of the opposite sex struck up a conversation. "We run a bed and breakfast in Portland."

"Do I detect a Midwest accent?"

Tawny batted her eyelashes. "We're originally from Ohio." She messed with her earring. "We don't have an accent."

"Most Midwesterners say they don't, when they clearly do. What sets you apart is the nasally way you pronounce vowels."

"We're not nasally."

The guy must've decided it was better not to argue. "We're delighted you came in." A large group seated themselves at a long table beside them, prompting their served to move on. "Enjoy your wine and cheese."

Tawny wouldn't let it go. "Do I sound nasally?"

"Stop obsessing. He was making conversation." Elaina took out her phone. "Steph and Grace will be bummed that we're here and they're not. Let's take a selfie and send it to them."

Their accents forgotten, she and Tawny made goofy faces and composed a text to go with the photo. '*Staying in Bangor overnight and possibly tomorrow night as well. Drinking wine. Eating mud cheese.*'

"Wow," Tawny said with a pinch of sarcasm, "for two single women in our forties, we lead exceptionally dull lives."

"How so?"

"Read back what you sent."

"Yeah, we are kind of boring."

"Instead of seizing the opportunity to search for hot men, we're in a dimly lit, albeit classy winery, hoping no one pays attention and nowhere in the text did we say we're going clubbing or doing anything else exciting."

Elaina ran the stem of her wine glass back and forth between her hands. "Your analysis could be correct."

"What do you mean could be? Of course it's correct. Let's find a hotel, make ourselves look irresistible, and paint the town red."

"Red, white, whatever."

"Definitely red – the color of seduction."

Laughing and trying to swallow at the same didn't go well. Wine spurted out of Elaina. "I should stick with water when you're around."

"And miss the burn when wine seeps out of your nose?" Tawny had a mirth on-off switch. She flipped the sucker off. "This was a much needed break from the madness that goes on at the hospital. My co-workers are great, but the situations that happen in an emergency room can knock your feet out under you," she snapped her fingers, "just like that. Did I tell you about the woman who accidentally put her hand through the glass in her storm door?" She shuddered. "It was gruesome."

"The poor lady."

"Blood doesn't make me queasy. Jagged torn flesh is another story."

They all needed to vent about the things that bothered them. Since the four of them seemed to be going in different directions these days, it was even more important to talk about what was going on in their heads. When it involved ripped skin, however, Elaina drew the line. "New subject."

"That's how I feel most days at the hospital. I want to hit that reset button so often."

"Maybe you should bid into the maternity unit. Cuddling babies would put you in a much better frame of mind."

"It's not just cuddling babies."

"I know. I'm trying to get rid of the grisly mind picture you painted with the storm door incident."

"I could see myself working in Labor and Delivery." Tawny bumped Elaina with the toe of her shoe. "Thanks for the suggestion. No one should work for long periods of time in the emergency room. Even though I haven't been there for a year, it still wreaks havoc on my brain."

"Forget painting the town red tonight. Instead, let's chill with another bottle of wine, Italian take-out from the restaurant next door, and vegging out in front of the TV."

Tawny did an over-the-top, drawn-out yawn. "No wonder there aren't any men standing in line to date us. We're two-legged snooze-fests."

"There might be men standing in line. We just can't see them."

Tawny moved Elaina's glass out of reach. "Stop the crazy talk."

Elaina fluttered her eyelashes and fanned herself with the drink napkin. "We could have hundreds of guys waiting to hear back from us on that dating site."

"You're hilarious."

"I might as well have fun with something that makes me ridiculously nervous."

Tawny smeared a cracker with goat cheese. "Don't think your heart wouldn't crack just a little if we checked the site and found zero interested parties."

"I'd be relieved."

"You say that now."

"I'm sincere." Elaina pointed to Tawny's cracker. "You were excited about goat cheese. Give it a taste."

Tawny brought the cheese laden cracker to her nose

and took a whiff. "Euw! It has a strong goatyness to it." She tossed the cracker back on the plate.

"What's happening to us, Tawn'? Saying no to goat cheese and searching for love online can only mean one thing – we've turned into wimps. When did that happen?"

Tawny tapped her chin. "Well, let's see, I'm about to celebrate the first anniversary of my divorce, so I've been a solid wimp for almost a year."

"You've dated and seemed to handle it fine."

"It's called acting. Beneath this confident façade lurks a major wimp. But please, I'm begging you – don't repeat what I just said, not even to Grace and Steph."

"I won't breathe a word, although, you recently pointed out that we're all in this together. Remember? Or does that only apply to when I want a secret kept? FYI, your wimpyness with regards to men is common knowledge. Anyone paying even a little attention knows you're apprehensive when it comes to love and romance. It's the same for me. Having your world turned upside down does that to a person. Some people don't rebound easily from bad situations, we happen to be two of them."

"Yet you told Jess Plainfield you loved him."

"A very unwise move, especially after he made it clear he didn't want to get involved. He was there to get his life together, and I screwed that up for him." Regret burned through Elaina instantly and rapidly, like someone had carelessly thrown a match into a sun-parched field of wheat stubble. She sighed and began to croon the lyrics from country superstar Lorrie Morgan's hit record, *What*

Part of No. But she switched them up a bit, "What part of no didn't I understand?"

"I can't fault you. I was attracted to Bartholomew Simpson and the flame went out pretty quick. I should've broken it off as soon as I realized things weren't working. Instead, I led him on so I wouldn't be the only one without a guy in my life. I hurt him."

"Maybe a little. I think your parting was mutual though. He wasn't feeling it either, Tawn'."

"Who would've thought life post-divorce would be so rough?"

"I compare it to someone spinning you around until you're dizzy and then letting go."

Tawny raised her glass in a toast. "To not letting anyone spin us. And to never ordering goat cheese again."

Chapter Five

~ Guard the cucumbers and watch out for bobbers! ~

Elaina put her phone on speaker while she primped in front of the mirror. It had taken Steph a while to respond to the text she'd sent earlier.

"You're staying in Bangor?" Steph whined.

Tawny made a goofy face at Elaina and answered Steph. "You and Grace made excuses not to come."

"I wanted to help Nick with food prep this morning at the restaurant."

"Key words: wanted to help. You chose Nick over us."

"Well duhhhh. He's a hunk. Why wouldn't I choose him over you?"

"I know this is a hard concept to grasp, but sometimes it should be besties over beefcake. Just saying." Tawny shoved the corkscrew into the cork of their newly acquired bottle of blackberry Merlot. It made a loud pop.

"What was that?"

"One of the best sounds a girl can hear on a Tuesday night."

"You can be a real pain, Tawn'."

"So I've been told."

"Elaina, it's your phone. Why are you letting that hooligan do all the talking?"

"Because I'm getting prettified."

"For what?"

"Tawny and I are going to enjoy a glass of wine and check out the Penobscot River Walkway."

"But we do wine on Wednesdays."

"Wine is good any night of the week."

"Hold on a sec." Steph shouted, "Grace, could you come here?"

"Man, you have a set of pipes. You didn't shatter every window in the house, did you?" Tawny taunted.

"Elaina, give her mean eyes for me." Steph yelled for Grace again.

Elaina and Tawny put hands over their mouths to smother their laughs.

Grace heeded the summons. "Why are you hollering? I was one floor up, not out in the garage."

Elaina acknowledged Grace with, "Hello."

Stony must've joined Steph and Grace. When he heard Elaina's voice he yowled. The sound of glass breaking was followed by Steph scolding him. "You broke my picture frame. Bad dog!"

"Stony didn't do it on purpose. He swished his tail and knocked it off your nightstand. You should dog-proof your room."

"Or I could ban him from my room."

"Go ahead. Let's see how that goes." Grace huffed out a sigh. "It's never-ending chaos at the Four Sassy Chicks Bed and Breakfast."

"We should put that on the sign out front," Elaina quipped to get their attention.

"So what's going on?"

"They're staying in Bangor and partying without us."

"You called me away from my book to tell me that? I thought you saw a mouse or fell and broke a hip. They're staying in Bangor. What's the big deal?"

"It's no big deal. It's just that I... Aww hell, I've got nothing."

"Where's Nick?" Tawny asked.

The thing actually bothering Steph emerged. "Late this afternoon, he flew to California with his son. They made an appointment to look at a vineyard in Napa County. Nick, II, wants to own and operate a winery. The one he's interested in is way out of his price range – or anyone's, for that matter. They called the realtor to get a private showing."

"Maybe it's just an excuse for a father-son getaway," Elaina offered.

"How much does this particular winery go for?"

"You don't want to know, Tawn'."

"It's a good thing I can't reach through the phone and flick you on the forehead, Steph. I wouldn't have asked if I didn't want to know."

"Don't collapse when I tell you it's listed at twenty-six million."

"Dollars?"

"No, cents."

"Twenty-six-million dollars?" Tawny said dryly. "That can't be right."

"Why do I bother talking to you?"

"You can't help yourself."

"Yeah, that's not it."

Tawny delved deeper. "What is Nick, II, thinking?"

"That he'd like his dad to pony up some money and go into business with him."

"Is Nicholas entertaining the possibility?"

"I don't know, maybe. He didn't say and I didn't ask." There was a slight quiver of something other than annoyance in Steph's voice.

"Is your boyfriend secretly a multi-millionaire?"

"If he is, it's a tightly guarded secret." Steph exhaled noisily. "The owner of the vineyard is originally from Italy and his home is fashioned after a villa he had near Tuscany. There are six additional buildings on the property. I think two are barns. The place comes with seven acres of premium vineyard, over a hundred fruit trees, and an expansive olive orchard."

"No doubt there are also three pools, two tennis courts, and an amphitheater. We should chip in and help Nick, II, buy it."

Steph's laugh was sarcastic. "You should do stand-up comedy."

"At the amphitheater of your new home? That would be cool."

"You're getting on my last nerve, Westerfield." Steph

directed a few questions to Elaina. She inquired about the hotel, their room number, and where they had dinner.

Elaina gave Steph the information, and added, "We might stay an extra day."

Steph continued to bellyache. "We should be with you."

"But you're not," Tawny stated with too much ha-ha in her tone. "Goodbye. We have wine to drink and men to chase." She ended the call.

"You need to ease up on Steph."

Tawny lifted her shoulders in a high shrug. "She dishes it out too."

"We all do. Did you hear the tremble in her voice?"

"She's not happy with us for being here without her."

"That much is true, yet there's more to it."

"You're not psychic."

"You don't know that." Elaina re-tied the laces on her sneakers. "Let's get our walk in."

* * *

"This is awesome." Tawny took a deep breath of clean, crisp air. "I'm glad you suggested we do this." She seemed to have the attention span of a gnat tonight. "Oh look, a food truck." Taking cash from her pocket, she headed to the truck. Over her shoulder, she let Elaina know they had chicken wraps. "I know I shouldn't indulge in more food after that big helping of veal parmigiana, but I like to support the locals wherever I go. It's a when-in-Rome kind of thing." She patted her belly. "Besides, I skipped the garlic bread."

When they were at the Italian restaurant, Tawny had eyed and drooled over the garlic bread for a good ten minutes. She'd told the gal working the take-out counter that she had to pass on the bread because she didn't want to go out tonight with horrendous breath. Elaina had exchanged an amused look with the gal.

Elaina passed on the wrap. The half-order of linguine Alfredo with shrimp and broccoli she'd eaten was more than enough to tide her over until breakfast. "Yeah, it's a when-in-Rome thing for me too." She ordered an iced tea.

They sat on a bench along the Penobscot River and watched boats go by.

Tawny picked at the wrap, eating only the chicken and tomatoes. "Maine is as close to heaven on earth as any place can get, yet there are days I long for Ohio."

"Me too. It was our comfort zone."

"You went back to Ohio to rescue Bailey. How did you feel when you were there?"

Elaina pondered the question. "I guess it temporarily filled a small void in my soul."

"You mentioned a while back that we should return to Cherry Ridge at some point due to all of us having unfinished business. At the time, I didn't understand where you were coming from – now I do."

"We left in a hurry and didn't get a chance to say goodbye in our own ways." Elaina liked this one-on-one time with Tawny. Deep conversations took place when it was just the two of them. The same thing happened when she was alone with Grace and had separate time with Steph as well. She loved when they were all together, but she also looked forward to hanging out with them individually. "I wasn't there long enough to pinpoint what kind of unfinished business I had. The trip involved a dog rescue, an uncomfortable and heart-wrenching visit with Arden, and falling head over heels for Jess."

"Speaking of Jess, have you texted him today?"

"After the brow-beating I got from you guys when you found out I was bugging him so much?"

"So that's a no?"

"It's a no." It was a sideways fib. She hadn't texted him, but she'd scoured his website for news about how his album was coming. In the banner across the top, it said the album would be delayed and apologized for the postponement, without offering a reason for the holdup. "As much as I hate to admit it, you made me see the error of my ways. Jess couldn't care less that I'm alive."

"I don't get it. He seemed into you." Tawny snapped her fingers. "What's the name of that song by Dr. Hook he made you listen to?"

"*A Little Bit More.* And he didn't make me listen to it; he wanted me to listen to it."

Tawny tapped the music app on her phone and searched her downloaded songs. "Here it is." She cranked up the volume so they could both enjoy it.

The romantic and sensual lyrics made Elaina sigh.

"That song was special to him and he conveyed his feelings for you through it."

"I thought so too. I also thought we had fire."

"It might not have been a bonfire, but there was

definitely a flame. We all saw it. There could still be embers. Maybe you should poke them."

"I poked them with text messages. He didn't poke back and you read me the riot act."

"I get that his main concern is his daughter's well-being. If I were in his shoes, I would've jetted to her side too. While he's trying to straighten out Alyssa, he shouldn't have to cut things off with you. That just doesn't make sense. There has to be another reason he's not responding."

Elaina rubbed her forehead. "Gordie asked about my love life. When I told him I didn't have one, he asked if I had trouble in the sack." Even though she and Jess hadn't gotten that far in their relationship, maybe she put off bad-in-the-sack vibes.

Tawny choked on a piece of chicken.

"Same reaction I had, minus the chicken."

* * *

Over the din of laughter and huddled conversations in the crowded bar, Elaina and Tawny discussed the insecurities they'd gone through as teenagers, that seemed to mysteriously crop back up almost the second they'd slipped off their wedding rings.

"At thirteen, I obsessed about the whiteness of my teeth." Tawny bared her chompers. "I still do, although I'm unwilling to give up things known to stain them." She moved her palms up and down like a scale. "White teeth or coffee? No-brainer."

Elaina had been alternating sips of water and Merlot. She held her wine glass up to the nautical-themed light fixture above their heads. "This might surprise you – white wine has more acid than red. The acid causes fine cracks in your enamel."

"How do you know this stuff?"

"My head's a trivia game waiting to be played."

"You're weird. That's why we get along so well." Tawny ran a finger over the slight crook in her lower front teeth. "I don't get why I fixated on the color of my teeth, when I should've been concerned with getting them straightened. My parents insisted on braces." Her brown eyes flared open a wee bit. "That was the first of many knock-down, drag-out fights I had with my folks. I didn't want a mouthful of metal. In hindsight, I was a colossal idiot. Stubbornness can be good sometimes; in most of my cases, not so much." Tawny's phone lay on the table near her fingertips. "I should call them and apologize for being a bad daughter."

"You weren't a bad daughter."

"I wasn't an easy one."

Elaina wet her lips with wine. "My scorecard wasn't filled with plus signs either."

"Samuels, I can't fathom you being bad. It's not in your DNA."

Elaina made a goofy face. "I'm no angel."

"Compared to me you are. Every day something jogs my memory about the handful I used to be."

"Used to be?" Elaina drew back in case Tawny decided to retaliate.

Tawny didn't strike back. Instead, she put her hands on her head. "All this self-reflection is cramping my brain."

"As long as we're doing a tell-all, I have a secret that may shock you."

Tawny propped her elbows on the table. "Go ahead, give it a try."

"In eighth grade, I was the only girl with no boobs."

"In no way is that shocking. At forty-four you're still the girl with no boobs."

"I've graduated from training bras, thank you very much." Elaina clicked her tongue. "One weekend a group of us went roller skating. There was a really hot guy I wanted to impress." She scoffed. "He ignored me to the point it drove me mad. I skated into the restroom, took off my socks, and rolled them into balls."

"You stuffed?"

"I absolutely did." Reliving the stupidity made Elaina giggle. "Thinking I pulled a fast one, I skated back into the crowd and stuck my chest out, hoping he would notice. He still didn't. My friends detected my sudden development right away though. In my haste to get out of the restroom, one of the socks had unrolled. I had one round boob and one deflated."

Tawny laughed so hard she almost fell off the high-rise pub chair.

"The teenage years. Ya gotta love 'em."

"Boobs aside, did you grow up having horrendous haircuts? My mom cut mine all the time and the result was one disaster after another."

Elaina used her fingers to imitate scissors. "My mom snipped my bangs and could never get them straight. She'd try to fix the unevenness. By the time she was done, they were almost to the top of my forehead. I looked silly until..."

Tawny interrupted. "After eighth grade?"

Elaina nodded. "No bangs. No boobs. Wow. I was a sight to behold. All my school pictures from kindergarten to high school have been locked in the vault and will never see the light of day until I need a good laugh."

"Your phone just rang."

"How could you hear it over this racket?" Elaina checked her phone. "I have a missed call from Grace. I'm going to pop outside to call her back."

The sidewalk in front of the pub was littered with people on their phones. Elaina wandered a half-block away for privacy. The cool night air made her shiver.

A souped-up sports car drove by slowly and someone from inside the vehicle wolf-whistled.

Elaina hadn't been whistled at in forever. Even though the flirtation was irrelevant, not to mention anonymous, it put a spring in her step.

Grace sounded out of breath when she answered her phone. "Where are you guys?"

"At a bar."

"Which one?"

Elaina looked over her shoulder to check out the sign of the bar. "Why?"

"Steph and I want to join you."

Elaina chuckled. "Via satellite?"

"You're a sad little clown. Give me the name so I can Google the location."

"What are you two up to?"

"Five-feet-four inches and five-feet-five inches, respectively."

"Now who's the sad little clown?"

"Enough jibber-jabber. We're at your hotel and you aren't."

Elaina was blown away. "You came to Bangor?"

"Umm, yeah. We couldn't let you and Tawny have all the fun, now, could we?"

"Tawny and I aren't exactly tearing up the town. We've indulged in some wine and talked about our teenage years."

"My kind of night. Any chance you'd want to continue *Elaina Samuels: The Teenage Years* at the hotel? I'm so ready to power down. Philip and I spent the day trying to remove wallpaper that's been stuck to the walls for years."

"Sucks to be you."

"Right?"

Elaina was happy that they'd come. "I'll grab Tawn' and we'll be there in fifteen minutes."

"On the way here, could you also grab some snacks? We didn't stop for dinner and we're starving."

"Consider it done."

An hour later they traipsed through the hotel parking lot, loaded down with purchases.

Steph met them at the revolving door of the hotel. "What took you so long? Grace was worried."

Grace sidled up and corrected the statement. "You were worried."

"You were too. I heard it in your voice."

Grace rolled her eyes and then rubbed her hands together. "What kind of goodies did you bring?"

Tawny lifted the bags for them to see. "Cucumbers, hot oil treatment, whitening strips, almond and honey hand scrub."

"Not the snacks I had in mind."

Elaina followed Tawny's lead and lifted her bags. "Spicy white tuna topped with avocado and wasabi mayo, edamame, California spring rolls, garlic shrimp, seared scallops, and French fries."

"Now you're talking."

Steph's forehead wrinkled. "All that yummy and you added fries?"

Tawny hip-checked Steph. "They're comfort food."

"Becausssssse?"

"Because I shouldn't have fought getting braces."

"Your communication strategy is still lost on me."

"I'm lost too." Grace looked at Elaina and mimicked bringing a glass to her lips. "A little too much vino?"

Elaina shook her head. "A little too much truth."

* * *

"Stop eating the cucumbers." Grace moved the paper plate out of Steph's reach. "They're to soothe our eyes."

Elaina came from the bathroom with her hair wrapped in a towel and white strips on her teeth. "Grace, it's your turn in the bathroom."

Grace handed Elaina the plate. "Guard the cucumbers."

Elaina broke into a wicked laugh. A whitening strip shot out of her mouth and landed on the cucumbers.

Steph made a face. "I'm not putting those on my eyes now."

"What's a little spit between friends?"

To ally herself with Elaina, Tawny took two cucumber slices, lay on the bed, and placed the veggies on her eyes. "The spit added a little something. These feel amazing."

Grace poked her head around the bathroom door. "This almond and honey hand scrub smells good enough to eat."

"Do a taste-test," Tawny joked.

Grace held out the jar, dipped in her finger and gave it a lick. She pretended to gag and made a bee-line for the sink.

"Not enough honey?" Elaina took a spot next to Tawny.

Grace peeked out of the bathroom again. "In small print it says: Not for human consumption."

Amusement vibrated between them, followed by an odd and utter silence.

Elaina closed her eyes and let the cucumbers do their thing. She inhaled contentment and exhaled the challenges of the day. Gordie and Ruth had been challenges, not big ones, but challenges none the less. The quirky couple had made her understand a few things; the most poignant – how great it was to be their age and still be in love. Would a love like theirs ever find its way into her life? She'd been under the illusion that she and Jess had the potential. In reality it had been a two-sided attraction and a one-sided love affair. Instead of tightening up over the analysis, she tried to rationalize that people come in and out of our lives for a reason. Maybe Jess had been put in hers as a walking, talking, handsome news bulletin to inform her that even after an unpleasant marriage she could still develop feelings for a member of the opposite sex. And maybe Gordie had been sent to deliver the message that she needed to explore the possibility she had 'trouble in the sack', and if so, fix it. Although how to make those kinds of repairs eluded her.

Tawny toed Elaina's ankle. "Why did you say 'hmm'?"

"I didn't realize I did." Elaina rolled to her side and whispered, "Just going over a few things in my head." Earlier she'd shared Gordie's question about her possible lack of prowess in the sack with Tawny. At the time, it didn't prompt a thorough discussion. That had to be a first. Usually a sensitive subject would've been dissected until there was nothing left to say.

"Such as?"

"Whether I actually have trouble in the sack."

Tawny's brows pinched together. "Are you referring to how you perform?"

Elaina's laugh was more of a scoff. "It's not a circus act."

"It could be." Tawny tried to hide a smile with her hand. "Do you lie still?"

"In all honesty, I may not be as active as other women."

"You do move though?"

"Yes, of course."

"Do you French kiss?"

"It's one of my favorite things." And it was about as personal as two people could get without getting full-on intimate. French kissing with Jess had been extraordinary. Elaina dug her fingernails into her palms. Constant thoughts about the musician would only make her more nuts.

"How about different positions?"

A jesting quip sprang forth of its own volition. "Like being the boss?"

"You're hopeless."

Steph flicked on the lamp. "What are you two whispering about?"

Elaina was grateful Tawny pulled a jack rabbit out of her bag of nonsense; although the particular rabbit she chose wasn't as helpful as it should've been. "Elaina's trying to drum up the nerve to check for messages on that dating site."

Under her breath, Elaina mumbled, "I'll get even with you."

Tawny's wink of mischief was followed by an elbow to her ribs. "I have no doubt."

In one fluid move, Steph was off the bed and had retrieved her laptop from the desk. "Let's get to it."

Elaina replied with dry sarcasm. "Let's not and say we did."

A flicker of bewilderment lit Steph's green eyes. "Do you want to check or not?"

"Not."

Tawny propped against the headboard. "She's such a flipper. One minute she's all about French kissing, the next she's a flounder flopping around on the bank."

The small amount confusion in Steph's gaze intensified. "That doesn't make sense."

"It doesn't have to. She's going to check her messages and I'm going to check mine. We're grown women who aren't afraid of anything."

"I'm afraid of yellow jackets buzzing around my head." Elaina's subtle wit earned her three glares.

Grace shrugged off the bed and stood in front of Elaina. "There aren't any yellow jackets in our room."

"Wanna bet?" Elaina volleyed her gaze between her three friends.

"Well then, check your messages or I'm going to sting you repeatedly."

"Coercion by friends – there ought to be a law against it." Elaina headed to the bathroom. "I'm going to wash the hot oil treatment out of my hair first. We're only supposed to leave it on for fifteen minutes – it's been twenty-five." She started to remove the towel wrapped around her head.

"A little while longer won't hurt." Grace latched onto Elaina's robe and steered her to the laptop.

"Okay, okay. Unhand me. I'm not going to bolt." Elaina sat at the desk, cracked her knuckles, and typed in her password. She held her breath and watched the dating site fill the screen. Four synchronized gasps rent the air when more messages than they could count popped up.

"See I told you." Tawny crowded into Elaina's space.

"Give me some breathing room, please."

"Only if you read aloud what all those possibilities have to say." Tawny put her hand over Elaina's to made her click into the first email.

In a sing-song voice, Elaina shared the details. "Bachelor number one likes long walks on the beach, sunsets, and gazing at stars. Give me a break."

"A little cookie-cutter, but he sounds nice. Go to number two."

Elaina cleared her throat. "Bachelor number two enjoys heart to heart conversations, also loves long walks on the beach, and ending the evening with coffee and dessert." She yawned to convey her opinion. "Bachelor number three...long walks...sunsets...yada yada. Guys must copy off each other or somewhere out there is a dating profile template."

"Don't get discouraged. One of them has to have an ounce of creativity," Grace said over Elaina's shoulder.

"Doubtful." Elaina shifted in the chair and read the next sixteen messages. Each one was strikingly similar to the first. "Last but not least – 'I enjoy the sound of water slapping into the rocky shoreline behind my home, long walks around the city to take in all the spectacular nuances that can only be seen on foot, music for slow dancing, light beer instead of dark ale, and women who are organized but don't get ruffled when an unexpected curve in the road throws off their carefully planned day.'"

"Holy mackerel!" Steph moved in closer, perhaps to

see if what Elaina had read was actually there or if she was making stuff up.

Elaina did a slow blink. "Not bad."

"Who is it?" Tawny crowded just as close as Steph.

"There's no name or picture, only initials."

Grace did a sweeping gesture with her hand. "And those initials are?"

Elaina brushed her fingers across the screen. "R.J.P."

Grace swiveled Elaina's chair around so she could look into her eyes. "I'm going to go out on a limb here and guess who those initials belong to."

"You'd be wrong."

"You decided that rather quickly."

Elaina pointed to the guys' information. "It says he lives in Ohio."

Grace squinted. "No it doesn't. It says he's from Ohio."

"It's not Jess."

Tawny grabbed Elaina's cell phone from the nightstand. "Dangle a carrot. Send him a text and ask if he likes to walk around the city on foot."

Steph agreed with Tawny and Grace. "Deep down, you know it's him."

Elaina mocked them with a scoff. "All three of your dipsticks are registering a quart low."

"Low on oil or not, three gut instincts can't be wrong. Don't you think it's odd that R.J.P. didn't post a picture? Yours is right there for the whole world to see, yet he chose to keep you guessing." Tawny flicked Elaina on the arm several times.

"It's not him. Why would Jess post a message on a dating site when he said he didn't want to get involved with anyone?"

Grace gave her two-cents. "Men need to come up with new material. The 'I have so much going on in my life right now I can't afford to get romantically involved' drivel has run its course. To be fair, for some guys that might be true – they could be overwhelmed with work, kids, or whatever. For others, it's just a way to get bedroom privileges without commitment. If that is Jess's bio," at Elaina's wince, Grace put her palms up, "I'm not saying it is, but for five seconds consider that it might be. It could mean his heart craves attention, even though he's stuck in Virginia. I'm sure he was just as shocked to find you on this site as you're shocked to find him."

Elaina held firm. "I'm telling you, it's not him."

Tawny didn't mince words. "The four of us swore an oath to tell each other like it is. Grace gave you an optimistic view. As you're well aware, I choose not to be PC. Here's my take – a lot of guys use the 'I can't get involved' excuse as a life preserver; the next day, you'll find them skinny dipping in the Atlantic with just their bobbers to hold them up, while they try to attract as many fish as possible."

"Their bobbers?" Laughter consumed Elaina at the visual Tawny had painted. She cackled and snorted until every ounce of mirth was spent. Sitting up straight, she exhaled a loud breath. "Give me my phone." She typed a quick text and tossed the phone on the bed. "Now we wait."

* * *

Grace's phone buzzed, stirring the four of them awake. "You've got to be kidding."

In the darkness, Steph moaned, "That has to be Cody."

Elaina popped open an eye. Cody was famous for calling in the middle of the night, even though Grace had pointed out to him the six hour time difference. It was currently three-thirty in the morning.

Tawny sat up against the headboard with a clunk. "You might as well find out what he wants."

Grace apologized for the inconvenience.

"There's no need to be sorry." There were notes of approval in Tawny's voice. "After you're done talking, we'll fall back asleep."

"If you're sure..."

Elaina, Tawny, and Steph said in unison, "We're sure."

"Uh, guys... He wants to Facetime."

Steph expelled a lengthy yawn. "Have at it, chick."

Grace flicked on the lamp. "I owe you."

"No you don't," Steph argued.

"Yes you do," Tawny chirped. "Buy us breakfast and we'll call it even."

"It's a deal." Grace accepted Cody's Facetime request. "Good morning, Son."

Cody spoke first in Italian. "Buongiorno, Mama. Good morning, Mom."

"You must have something important to share since

it's the wee hours of the morning in Maine."

Cody filled the screen of Grace's phone with an ear to ear grin and then backed up to make Isabella and Karina visible. "Actually, we do have something to share."

There was a lot of clatter going on in the background.

"Where are you?"

"At the obstetrician's office."

Grace motioned for Elaina, Tawny, and Steph to huddle close. "Is everything going okay with your pregnancy, Isabella?"

"It's going well." Isabella turned to Cody and said, "Portresti dirglielo."

Cody gave Isabella a quick kiss on the mouth and then pecked the top of Karina's head with a soft smooch. Karina giggled. "Isabella wants me to tell you she had an ultrasound done today. The baby is healthy and growing." He held up a copy of the ultrasound. "See?"

Grace shouted, "Yessss!" and slapped her hands across her heart. In the process, the phone tumbled to the floor. "Oh no!"

Elaina retrieved the phone and handed it to Grace. "You're in the luck. They're still there, smiling like a beautiful, happy family."

"Cody, Isabella, Karina," tears leaked from Grace's eyes, "I'm so excited! I can't wait to meet the little one."

"The doctor thinks the baby will arrive sometime around early to mid-August."

"I'm not sure I can wait that long."

The connection dropped out, but came back on right away.

Elaina offered congratulations. Tawny and Steph took turns doing the same. "We're going to give you some privacy. Girls, don your robes. We're heading to the lobby."

Tawny bent down and asked Cody, "Does the ultrasound show a bobber?"

Grace chuckled.

"A bobber?" The question must've answered itself once Cody said it out loud. "Oh. Right. We can't see a penis anywhere in the picture. That doesn't mean there isn't one. It might be camera shy."

Tawny gave Grace a half-hug. "Your son is a chip off the ole block."

"Come on, troublemaker." Steph tried to guide Tawny away. Of course, Tawny resisted.

"I can't go downstairs looking like the bride of Frankenstein. Look at my hair."

"You do have a bad case of bed-head, but hey, on you it works."

"Sure it does. See what I have to put up with, Cody?"

Elaina took one of Tawny's arms and Steph took the other. "Have a nice chat. Bye Cody, Isabella, and Karina."

Grace blew them a kiss.

In the hallway, Tawny lurked on her tiptoes and peered around corners like she was part of an undercover operation. At the elevator, she loudly said, "It's all clear."

Steph shook her head. "You're a dork to the nth degree."

Tawny was startled when the elevator doors opened and two maintenance men walked out.

The men didn't say a word about their state of dress. In their line of work, they probably witnessed odd behaviors at all hours of the night.

When they reached the lobby, Steph went to the desk and apologized for intruding into the quiet.

The guy behind the counter was busy printing off invoices that would be slipped under the guests' doors sometime before the sun came up. "No problem. I just made a fresh pot of coffee if you're interested."

"We'll pass, but thank you. We're just killing time while our friend Facetime's with her son."

The hotel clerk gave Steph an obligatory smile and continued to work.

Steph wandered to an oversized comfy chair and snuggled into it.

Elaina and Tawny checked out a brochure of things to do in Bangor.

"There's Stephen King's house. Look at the wrought iron fence. It has gargoyles on it." Tawny tapped the page. "We have to do a photo op in front of it. Then we'll make an 11" x 13" print and hang it next to the semi-naughty portrait Philip did of us."

"I still can't believe we posed for that painting." Elaina continued to scan the brochure.

"We call our business Four Sassy Chicks Bed and Breakfast. With a name like that, our guests expect something unusual and fun. The risqué picture stays and the photo shoot in front of Stephen King's house will happen."

"Also on the agenda for today, we'll visit the huge

statue of Paul Bunyan. It could be another photo op."

Tawny arched an eyebrow. "He wasn't really that big, you know."

"It matters not. We're going."

Steph uncurled from the chair. "You have to take us to the winery that had goat cheese. After that, we have serious shopping to do."

"I hate shopping."

"You'll have to suck it up, Tawn'. Grace's grandbaby is going to need a few things. Bobber or no bobber, it'll be fun."

Chapter Six

- Things aren't always as they seem! -

"Spur of the moment trips are the best."

"I agree, G.G." Elaina smiled to herself. Grace had been on cloud nine since she'd Facetime'd with Cody. The baby shopping trip had warmed her heart. Essentially, it had been a mini baby shower. Tawny bought a stroller with all the bells and whistles. With the flick of a few levers, it converted to an infant car seat. Steph fell in love with a stuffed elephant that would've taken every bit of car space to transport home. Her bottom lip jutted out when Grace said a firm, "No." Steph compromised with a small mama elephant and two babies. Elaina asked which diaper bag Grace preferred and that became her purchase. Grace had gone crazy with clothes shopping for the little one. She left the store with three bags stuffed with sizes zero to six months.

"G.G.," Grace repeated. "Might I ask what it stands for?"

"Grandma Grace."

"It has a nice ring to it." Grace sat on the purple beast and kicked her legs back and forth with a distant look in her eyes. "Can I divulge something that's been bothering me?"

"You can tell me anything, you know that."

Grace pulled at her bottom lip with her teeth and stretched her neck from side to side. "I'm so grateful to be blessed with grandchildren. What I'm about to say though, will sound as though I'm not."

Elaina offered a theory. "At forty-two, being called grandma makes you cringe?"

Grace's light blue eyes widened. "Am I that obvious?"

"Not at all."

"Then how did you know?"

Elaina shrugged.

Grace puffed out a breath. "Am I shallow?"

"Don't be so hard on yourself. What you're feeling is a temporary reaction. The second you hold that tiny miracle, you'll be a goner." Elaina fanned her hands out. "I can see you wearing a *Greatest Grandma on the Planet* t-shirt. You'll be telling the cashier at the grocery store that you're a grandma. The gal at the airport reservation desk will have her ear bent with a grandma story. You'll show baby pictures to every guest we have."

Grace left the gothic loveseat to give Elaina a hug. "Thank you. You always set my world right. Instead of owning a bed and breakfast, you should've become a therapist."

"And miss all this?" Elaina looked around the huge living room. She made an imaginary picture frame with her hands. "I'm caught up in artwork these days. That

Paul Bunyan picture will look fantastic between the recliners."

"Your taste in art is wacked."

"What? You don't think a picture of us in front of that giant lumberjack is art?"

"The gal you asked to take our picture with your phone took one picture and didn't check to make sure it was good."

"It's good. In fact, it's spectacular."

"All four of us blinked."

Elaina scrolled through the photos on her phone and found the picture. She showed it to Grace. "The picture is definitely wacked...and it's going on the wall."

Grace cocked her head. "How can you be nonchalant and open-minded about some things, and closed off when it comes to certain other things?"

"Such as?" Elaina had a hunch where Grace was headed.

"Online shopping."

"I shop online all the time."

"That's not the kind of shopping I meant."

"For men?"

Grace directed a finger at Elaina. "Bingo."

Elaina exhaled a loud breath and relocated her gaze to the floor. "I shopped. Nothing caught my eye. Besides, I don't buy unless it's on sale." She laughed at her sad attempt at humor.

"What are you afraid of?" Grace quickly added, "Besides yellow jackets circling your head."

Elaina's head snapped up at the thought-provoking

question. "I don't know, maybe I'm afraid the rejection will hurt more than I'm prepared to patch."

"We grow from the things that don't go according to plan."

"If that's the case, I'm six foot tall by now. Arden. Michael. Chad. Jess. None of those relationships went right."

"Yeah, I'm puzzled by the whole Jess thing. You seemed perfect for each other."

"He's walled me off, Grace. The line I cast about the dating profile is still in the water."

"Maybe he's embarrassed that you found him there. Or maybe he's just a douche."

* * *

When the phone rang for the fifth time in less than an hour, Elaina almost lost her balance on the three-rung ladder she stood on to clean the cabinets.

"Four Sassy Chicks Bed and Breakfast. This is Elaina. How can I help you?"

A soft-spoken female stated she'd seen their website and especially noted pets were allowed.

"We love pets. In fact, we have two dogs in residence – a sweet Siberian Husky named Stony and a feisty Pomsky we call Bailey."

"I can't wait to meet them."

Elaina waited for the caller to say more. When she hit dead airspace, she asked, "Would you like to make a reservation?"

"I would. This is short notice, but is tomorrow too soon?"

"Tomorrow works fine."

There was another significant pause in the conversation.

"Elaina, I need to tell you something upfront."

"You don't have a llama or giant peacock, do you?"

A small laugh filtered through the phone line. "No llamas, no peacocks. Linus is a sweet dog with a special type of behavior. He's not an official service dog, but he's protective and keeps me calm."

It didn't really tell Elaina anything about why Elizabeth needed to be upfront.

The phone beeped with an incoming call. "Can I put you on hold for a second?"

"Certainly."

"Four Sassy Chicks Bed and Breakfast. This is Elaina. How may I help you?"

"Oops. I was trying to reach someone else." A man apologized and ended the call.

Elaina had her finger to the button to return to the first call when the phone beeped again. She repeated the standard greeting. It was the same person with the wrong number.

"How in the world did I get you twice?" The guy shared the number he'd dialed.

"Our number ends in five."

He laughed. "Small phone, big fingers. Again, my apologies."

"Have a good day." Elaina went back to the original

call. "Sorry for the wait. We'd be tickled to have you and your dog."

A sigh of relief was followed by a handful of thank-you's. "He won't be a problem, I promise." The caller introduced herself as Elizabeth and said she recently retired from the Connecticut school system after forty years of teaching. With the arrival of spring, she and her dog planned to visit the rest of New England and work their way west.

Elaina thanked Elizabeth for being a teacher and offered congratulations on her retirement.

"It's been a rewarding journey. Now it's time to do something different. All the places I taught my students about in Geography class are on my itinerary."

Elaina inquired if Linus was up to date on his immunizations and kennel cough vaccine.

"We made a trip to the vet yesterday. He's good to go."

"Will you require transportation from the airport?" Connecticut wasn't far from Maine, yet some people preferred flying versus driving.

"Actually, I bought a van so Linus will have room to move. I'm glad you can put us up on such short notice. Portland wasn't on our itinerary, but I thought it over and decided I didn't want to subject him to too many miles on the first leg of our trip."

Elaina was about to ask for credit card information to secure the room when Elizabeth said she had to go.

"I'm in line at the grocery with a bag of dog food. I came close to dropping it and my phone three times.

The guy in front of me isn't happy that I'm holding a conversation so close to him. He's turned around twice and given me a how-rude eyebrow. I don't make a habit of talking on my phone in public places, yet this time it couldn't be helped. I have to go." Elizabeth abruptly ended the call without letting Elaina get in a word edgewise.

Steph flounced into the kitchen dressed in her coat, hat, and gloves. "I'm headed to the restaurant to do food prep. Later, I'll pick up Nick and his son at the airport. I can't wait to hear about their trip to Napa."

"Did they buy the winery?" Expecting a flat out "no", Elaina was mystified when Steph said she had no idea.

"I asked, and Nick deflected by saying he wanted to do a taste-and-see experiment tonight with friends."

"Hmm to the dodge. Another hmm to the experiment."

"He's being mysterious and I don't like it. If they bought the winery, he should just tell me. I think he's trying to sidetrack me with busy work so I can't grill him."

"I take it the experiment has to do with your cookbook?"

Steph lifted her shoulders. "At this point, who the heck knows?"

Elaina wrenched Steph in a half-hug. "Don't worry. Nick's a great guy. He wouldn't blind-side you with a sudden relocation the way Jack Kirby did. I'm sure that's in the back of your mind though."

"You put that together too?"

Elaina silently groaned at her propensity to resurrect things that should remain in the past. The mention of Jack would only make Steph more anxious and suspicious of Nicholas's behavior. "I'm sure Nick has a good reason for not bringing you up to speed. Tonight's food experiment might tie into it somehow."

Steph clenched and unclenched her hands. "Nick seems to genuinely care. I've been telling myself to be patient and when the time is right, he'll unveil what's next for us."

"That's a positive frame of mind."

"Elaina, there's also this niggling voice in my head that fills me with doubt. It makes me question if beneath all Nick's sweetness lurks the heart of a jackal. He could be stalling the information about California because he hasn't figured out how to tell me he's starting over... without me."

"This isn't déjà vu and Nick isn't a jackal."

"How do you know? None of us are experts when it comes to men."

"Intuition is our superpower, Steph. We get signs along the way, not just regarding men. Sometimes we tune into them and sometimes not. You got a feel for Nick right away. Deep down you know he's decent. You wouldn't have him living under this roof, if he weren't."

Exasperation gushed out of Steph. "Why are relationships so hard?"

"As a rule, they aren't. Once you've been hurt, though, your defense mechanisms are always at the ready. One suspicious move, they kick in."

"So what do I do?"

"Be brave."

"That's all you've got?"

"I could get philosophical and give you the nothing-worth-having-comes-easily speech."

Tawny came in from the garage with a bag of groceries. "Who's easy?"

Without a breath of hesitation, Elaina made it clear she wasn't easy.

Tawny suggested she add that to her dating profile.

"What dating profile?"

Tawny took two cans of coffee from the grocery bag. "Did you take it down?"

"Who has time for dating? Pandemonium will soon descend upon us – in a good way." Elaina shoved the reservation ledger across the counter for Steph and Tawny to peruse.

Tawny pointed to the entry Elaina had circled. "Who's Linus?"

"He's coming tomorrow."

"Would I like him?"

Elaina's mouth split into a grin. "I'm counting on it."

* * *

"We'd like to show off what we've done to the place. Keep in mind it's not close to being finished." Philip took a step toward the front door, with a hopeful look on his face.

"Nick and I would love to see all your hard work.

Our curiosities will have to be put on hold though until tomorrow. Tonight we're doing a thing at the restaurant." Steph looked at her watch. "We have to set up in a half hour."

"And you didn't invite us?" Philip pretended to be hurt.

"It's to rally interest for our cookbook." Steph slid her gaze to Elaina.

Elaina gave her a small nod.

Philip wouldn't let it go. "I'm interested in your cookbook."

Grace jabbed him with her elbow. "Back off, Treatwood. Steph and Nick have some catching up to do – without us."

Philip stated that Steph looked tense and asked if everything was okay.

Steph moaned. "I hope so."

Nick descended the stairs, smiling and straightening his tie.

"Augustine, what did you do?"

Nick's carefree attitude morphed into a puzzled frown. "You'll have to be more specific."

Grace whispered, "Stop meddling."

Philip said in his usual loud tenor, "I'm not meddling."

Grace pinched his love handle.

"Oww."

Nick set eyes on Steph. "What's this about?"

"Philip wanted us to see the progress they've made on their house. I told him we couldn't tonight."

Nick squinched his eyes half-way closed and instead

of prodding Steph for a better answer, he went to Philip. "Why do you think I did something?"

Elaina jumped into the conversation with both feet, trying to hinder the inquiry. "We'll have an unusual guest tomorrow."

With his eyes still narrowed, Nick replied, "What does that have to do with anything?"

"She's trying to save me from having to explain Philip's buttinski question, that's what." Steph crossed her arms. "I'm concerned, Nicholas Augustine, that you're being evasive. You've said the bare minimum regarding the winery. Are you leaving Maine and moving to California?"

Steph had taken Elaina's suggestion to be brave. A tiny part of Elaina wished she hadn't encouraged the boldness.

Nick studied Steph. "This should be a private conversation."

"That was my intention all along."

Grace pinched Philip again.

"Sorry, guys, this is my fault. Grace tried to stop me from putting my nose where it didn't belong."

Nick helped Steph with her coat. "On our way to the restaurant, we'll talk."

Steph whimpered her way out the door. Nick followed without making eye contact with anyone.

No one breathed until they were sure Steph and Nick were gone.

Grace lit into Philip. "I'm not happy with you right now!"

"How did I know I was treading into murky waters?"

"You can't be that thickheaded. When I told you to let it go, that should've clued you in."

Philip's sheepish grin didn't diminish Grace's irked expression.

"I sensed Steph was in distress and wanted to help."

Grace softened in an instant. "You should assess the situation first, and then decide whether it's appropriate to render help."

"Actually, Philip, you did great." Tawny patted him on the back.

Grace frowned at Tawny's differing opinion.

Tawny explained that Steph would've stewed all night if Philip hadn't forced things out into the open. "Did you see her stand up to Nick?"

Elaina sat in a recliner. "Nick can't dodge Steph any longer. He has to tell her what he's up to."

Grace raised her palms. "I concede. They're right." She gave Philip a firm look. "That doesn't give you carte blanch to interfere whenever you darn well please."

"Noted." He picked Grace up and swung her around.

"Put me down."

Elaina's cell phone plinked from the kitchen counter where it sat charging. She was out of the chair and on the run.

"I'll bet it's R.J.P. answering your text."

Elaina hoped Tawny was right. She grabbed her phone, rushed to the bathroom, and locked the door.

Instead of Tawny, Grace, and Philip bugging her to know about the text message, Stony and Bailey decided to become pains. Stony yowled and Bailey yipped for her to open the door.

Elaina ignored them and focused on the message – *'I need you. Please come right away. I can't explain over the phone. Book a flight and I'll pick you up at the airport.'* Placing the phone on the sink, she covered her face with her hands and muffled a groan. Go? Don't go? After collecting herself, she traipsed out to the living room and pasted on a smile.

"Ah ha! It was Jess."

Elaina didn't confirm the accuracy of Tawny's guess. "Grace, I know you and Philip want to keep working on your place to make it livable, but I need a favor. Could you fill in for me for a day or two? Elizabeth and Linus are set to arrive tomorrow. I'll check in with you, in case you have questions." She sprinted toward the basement.

Tawny caught up and put a hand on the door to keep it from being opened. "You're leaving?"

Elaina wouldn't reveal anything, per his wishes. "I'm making a quick trip, yes. Would you help Grace out as much as your schedule permits?"

"Elainaaaa, did Jess decide he can't live without you?"

She wouldn't outright lie. "That remains to be seen."

"It was him on the dating site, wasn't it?"

Again, Elaina wouldn't verify Tawny's assumption. She took Tawny by the shoulders and moved her out of the way. "I'll give you an answer once I find out myself."

"Fair enough."

In her bedroom, Elaina paced. He needed her? For what? She stared so hard at her phone it felt like her eyes crossed. Blowing out a stout breath, she made a decision. *'I'll send you my flight information once I get it from the airline.'*

She received an immediate response, like he couldn't wait to hear from her. *'Thank you.'*

That's it? Thank you?

His lack of details made her nervous.

'Can you give me a hint what this is about?'

'I'd rather say it in person.'

Okay then. Elaina would sort out the rightness or wrongness of her actions on the way. She tossed a few things into an overnight bag, made sure she had cash in her wallet, and took the steps two at a time to get back upstairs.

Tawny, Grace, and Philip were huddled together.

Philip winked. "Good luck."

"You don't need luck. You've got this, Elaina." Grace took her by the arm and led her to the garage. "Have fun."

Tawny followed and smoothed a hand over Elaina's back. "I hope things turn out the way you want them to."

Elaina smiled through her uncertainty. "I'll be back soon."

Grace said to keep them informed.

And just like that, Elaina was on her way to Portland International Jetport. On Jetport Boulevard, she took her foot off the gas and putted slowly toward the airport. A car behind honked, urging her to get the lead out. Instead, she pulled into a hotel parking lot across from the airport and shut off the engine.

Laying her head back against the headrest, she watched a jet take off and another one land. The tiny voice inside prompted her to stop over-thinking things and to just go.

Three plinks of her phone indicated a trio of incoming messages. "If you've changed your mind and are telling me to stay put for now, I'll stay put all right – I won't leave Maine, even if you get on your knees and beg." Risking insanity, Elaina checked the phone. To her surprise, none of the texts were from him. Tawny, Grace, and Philip were trying to get the juicy particulars.

Compiling a group message, Elaina included Steph. As soon as it indicated delivery, she turned off the phone.

Chapter Seven

- Never say never! -

Seeing the man who could reduce her to rubble with just a look sent a rush of dread over Elaina.

Tall, dark, and broodingly handsome, Arden Samuels' head snapped from person to person as they made their way past the last security check-point and into the baggage claim area.

Elaina did an about-face.

A TSA agent stood with his feet shoulder width apart and hands on his hips. He shook his head, warning she couldn't return to the secure area.

Elaina did an exaggerated stretch to look at the bookstore a hundred feet behind him. "I'd like to buy a book."

He didn't have to say a word; his unyielding frontage of professionalism said he wouldn't make an exception.

"I see my ex-husband in the lobby and I'd rather not face him. If you know anything about exes, every time you see them it's like ripping off a scab along with some fresh skin."

The man didn't blink.

Elaina expelled a lengthy sigh. "Keep up the good work and have a nice day." She wanted to smack her forehead repeatedly for coming to Dayton to meet Arden. He hadn't said why he wanted her there and she hadn't pressured him for the reason. He'd sounded frantic and she'd dropped everything to come. It was the second time in a few months she'd come to Ohio for him. She could've easily told him to own whatever catastrophe he'd caused and handle it himself. But, whether she liked it or not, Arden Samuels would always be a special...butthead. Most women would've blanked him out of their lives, and when he asked for help, they would've laughed their heads off and followed up with strong language. She did neither and it made her a special kind of butthead, too.

Sucking in a deep breath, she squared her shoulders and marched toward whatever the heck this might be.

Arden spotted her and his grim expression changed to a half-smile.

Elaina glanced over her shoulder to the TSA agent. He also wore what appeared to be a half-smile. If she didn't know better, she'd swear he and Arden were friends.

"Thank you for coming, Elaina." Arden surprised her with a tight hug. That was so not him.

Pushing out of the embrace, Elaina took a step back. "What's wrong? Why did you want me here?" She had a sinking feeling that things weren't working out between him and Rachel. Any second he'd start bellyaching about women and their expectations.

Arden took her overnight bag from her hand. "Let's

go somewhere for coffee and I'll fill you in."

Ten minutes later they were seated at a café down the road from the airport. Elaina had ordered a grilled chicken wrap and a mocha latte topped with whip cream. Arden bypassed food and went straight for a large espresso.

Elaina sipped her latte and licked the whip cream from her lips, suspicious that Arden hadn't ridiculed her for bingeing on something filled with sugar and caffeine. He hadn't winced dramatically or huffed out a sigh like he was known to do when he wanted to convey displeasure. Then again, he wasn't exactly following his golden rule about putting only the good stuff in your body, and since it was well-past dinner time the massive caffeine in his drink was sure to keep him awake all night. "I'm on pins and needles here." Again, she braced for criticism for trying to rush him. To her shock, watery emotion clouded his eyes. "Arden?"

In the span of a breath, he fell apart. Tears fell hard and fast from his eyes, and he made no effort to stop them.

Elaina left her side of the booth and scooted next to him. "Talk to me."

He plunged his face into her shoulder and sobbed.

Arden Wellby Samuels never cried. In one of their many fights, Elaina had accused him of having his tear ducts removed. Obviously, she'd been wrong. This wasn't the guy she'd been married to. The Arden she knew mocked people who showed excessive sentiment in public. Yet here he was, weeping in a café.

Scenarios played out in her head – he'd lost his millions, Rachel got tired of being dominated and threw him to the curb, he missed Neil a.k.a. Bailey and wanted her returned, the home she'd sold back to him possibly had lost its value due to the dog hair left behind by Stony...or a termite invasion. What else could it be? From out of the blue, she asked, "Did you find out that Rachel's having triplets?"

Arden's head zinged up. Pain filled his red-rimmed eyes. "She...she..." He was overcome again and couldn't finish his thought.

Elaina touched his cheek. "Tell me what you're going through."

Arden sniffed, cleared his throat, and swiped at more tears. "Rachel has cervical insufficiency."

Elaina took his hand and held it, while scrambling to consider what cervical insufficiency entailed.

He answered the unspoken, burning question. "She's at risk to lose the baby."

"Ohhh, Arden, I'm so sorry."

"We can't lose this child. We just can't."

The day she'd rescued Bailey from his clutches, he and Rachel had announced they were having a baby. Elaina had been consumed with a type of grief at the news because Arden had denied her the privilege of becoming a mother, but she'd come to accept it wasn't meant to be for her. Now, she was just as distraught, but this time for them. "What did the doctor say?"

"That Rach' might go into premature labor or miscarry. He gave her meds meant to strengthen her cervix and confined her to bed. Nothing says either will work." Arden hung his head. "This is my fault. My fault," he repeated mournfully.

Elaina put her hand under his chin and raised his head so they were eye to eye. "How could this possibly be your fault?"

His voice trembled, "It's payback for me being a jerk for years."

The manager of the café started toward them and Elaine gave him a subtle shake of her head to keep him away.

Customers stared while waiting in line for their orders.

Regardless of where they were, Arden Wellby Samuels was in major pain, and he needed to express himself. As much as Elaina didn't want to care, how could she not? "This isn't karma, Arden."

"It has to be. Why else would this be happening?"

"Pregnancy complications aren't uncommon. Arden, her doctor identified the issue and is taking steps to give the baby more time to further develop and grow." Elaina squinched her brows together. "Why are you here, instead of at home with Rachel?"

"No one else understands why I'm so upset, but I knew you would."

That wasn't an answer. Elaina made the sound of a buzzer going off. "Try again."

Arden ran his fingers back and forth across his forehead. "I was nasty to the doctor and now Rachel's livid. She told me to leave."

"You left her alone?"

"Her mom is with her."

Elaina wanted to smack him upside the head. "Rachel and the baby are your responsibility. You should be there, not your mother-in-law. And when I say be there, I mean waiting on your wife hand and foot."

"You must have wax-buildup in your ears, so I'll say it again – she told me to leave."

"Ooooh. Ouch. Wax-buildup." Elaina stopped picking at her chicken wrap and proceeded to poke him in the chest with her finger. "In spite of Rachel's anger, you need to be with her every step of this pregnancy. Prove to her...and to yourself...that you're all-in when it comes to your marriage and fatherhood. Don't be an okay support system, be a great support system. Stop fighting with the love of your life, and start sucking up to her. You could do some damage control with the doctor too, by apologizing for your bad behavior and by making a donation in his name to the hospital where Rachel will deliver."

"You always go overboard."

Elaina's temper rose to the surface. She held most of the anger at bay; a little slipped out in her tone. "I'm serious! Step up." Part of her wanted to add, "You rat bastard." But name-calling would shut him down and the travel to Ohio would've been in vain. "She's relying on you to see her through this crisis. Bullying her doctor will escalate the stress she's under."

"I'm stressed too."

"I know you are, but at this critical juncture it's all about her. Get it?"

Arden sat back with a look of astonishment, like he couldn't believe she was mouthing off to him. Or the truth finally sank in. He sat wordless for a good minute. "You're right. I've made this more about me than Rachel. Truthfully, I've been fighting this whole father-thing because I…"

Elaina looked around, thinking he clammed up because he'd spotted someone he knew. She didn't see anyone other than the café employee. The other customers had taken their orders to go. A random flick from her intuition penetrated her heavy thoughts with clarity. "You're afraid."

A large divot creased the small space between his eyebrows.

"You don't think you're afraid of anything. Well guess what? For once in your life, you're terrified of not knowing what to do." Before Arden could go into a defensive rant, Elaina rested a hand on his arm to stop him. "This isn't criticism. It's an observation. Things have to go a certain way, or you get tense." Smoothing a hand up and down his shirt sleeve, she spoke softly and without condescension. "Life is filled with curves, detours, and traffic jams. Circumvent the traffic jam in your head, and exercise some patience. Go home to Rachel. Go home to the child that needs extra-care. And for the love of God, tell me the real reason why I'm here, because I don't have a clue. For years, you shoved me away."

Arden cleared his throat three times. "You're…" Again, he curbed his thought.

"Don't hold back. I'm a big girl. I can take it."

He hem-hawed again, but finally said, "You're positive energy."

Of all the things she thought he'd say, that wasn't it. "Thank you, I think."

"I mean it, Elaina. You try to see the bright side of everything. I didn't appreciate your candidness and optimistic views back then. I do now. I'm sorry it's taken so long."

Emotion welled up inside Elaina. She had to force it back down. What didn't happen between her and Arden was ancient history and she no longer wanted to cry about the past. It was hard to admit that each visit with the egghead seemed to heal her a little more. "We're okay, Arden. Really. Now get your keister home. Rachel and baby-to-be are waiting." Elaina stood and shrugged into her coat. "Nix the word fight from your thoughts and actions, and work at being happy."

Arden slid out of the booth. "I will. I'm going to be a dad – a damn good one."

Elaina forearmed him. "A good husband, too."

"Absolutely."

"Excellent. My work here is done." That sounded cheesy, but hopefully true.

"From the bottom of my heart, thank you for coming. You didn't have to, yet you did, and I'll be forever grateful. I promise not to bother you until the baby's born. I'll send you a picture."

"I'd like that." Elaina stepped on her tiptoes and pecked his cheek with a kiss. "Take care."

Arden latched onto her wrist. "Not so fast. I wanted to ask you something. It's a sensitive question. You don't have to answer, but I hope you will. Do you have someone special?"

Thoughts of Jess sprang into Elaina's mind. She raised her chin and pushed a broad smile into her face. "I definitely do – Tawny, Steph, and Grace."

* * *

With a Chef salad from room service in her lap, Elaina sat up against the headboard. She'd barely touched the chicken wrap earlier, but it would've been heartless to concentrate on food when Arden had been so distraught. And now her stomach was growling every couple seconds to remind her she hadn't eaten much all day. Dragging a piece of lettuce through a puddle of dressing, she brought the fork to her mouth, but then laid it back down. She was still mentally caught up in how things had played out with Arden. His transformation from ogre to decent human being was one for the history books. Tawny, Grace, and Steph would never believe it. Even she had difficulty trusting that it had happened.

Elaina eyed her phone setting on the nightstand. It had been shut off for several hours and she was going to get an earful from her friends. She powered the phone back to life. All the messages sent while she was unavailable rushed into her inbox faster than a freight train in the wide open spaces.

Elaina scrolled to the first one, sent by Tawny.

'*Dayton? Are you freaking kidding me? If you're not, I'm making an appointment for you to see a therapist. You fly off to see your ex-husband whenever he decides you should be there. I can't wrap my head around that, Elaina. Did the barracuda get another pet and decide it was too much trouble? Perhaps a goldfish? Or an otter? I love animals, but the second you bring home an otter I'm out of here. Kidding!!! I'm sure you get the gist of what I'm saying.*'

Elaina did a quick search for unusual house pets and sent this response to Tawny. '*Barracudas eat fish, gold or otherwise. What's your take on ferrets?*' She laughed and went on to the next message, this one from Steph.

'*Nick and Nick, II, will continue to reside in Maine! Woohoo! Picture me happy! The winery in California was a temptation they had to resist. The down payment alone scared them back to reality. Guess why Nick was being mysterious – they found a winery outside Portland for sale. If they buy it, we should name it The No Sweat Pants Allowed – Wine Club. What do you think? By the way, the impromptu taste-and-see event was a hit. One of the invited guests was a food critic. Nick kept it a secret so I wouldn't be nervous. Why did you go to Dayton? I won't judge, just curious.*'

"I can always count on you to make me smile, Steph." Elaina ate half her salad and sent a reply. '*The two of you may find yourselves one day in Napa Valley, but for now, I'm delighted that you'll remain in the Pine Tree State for a while longer. Anything involving wine and sweat pants is sure to be a success – just saying. Now all you have to do is convince Nick. Haha!*' Elaina added a row of laughing emojies. *'I can't wait to hear what the critic had to say.'*

Next up, a message from Grace, who kept things light too. *'What did the infamous ex want this time? His closets organized? Love you and hurry back.'*

The sassy chicks had also sent an assortment of side comments after their initial messages:

Tawny – *'You should change your phone number so he can't reach you.'*

Steph – *'Arden doesn't get that you're no longer his.'*

Grace – *'You still have yet to tell us about Linus. Is he hot?'*

Tawny – *'Steph is making some kind of weird carrot salad. Tell her to stop. LOL'*

Instead of a one-on-one message, she put together another group text to cover them all. *'Don't bug me. I'm going to catch some Zzz's early. I have to be at the airport at five o'clock. See you noon-ish tomorrow.'*

Tawny had to have the final word. *'With or without a ferret?'*

Elaina purposely left the inquiry unanswered. *'The carrot salad sounds interesting.'*

* * *

"I was starting to think Arden kidnapped you."

Elaina mocked Grace with a playful eye roll. "Why would he abduct me? I'm not his type."

"When you were married, you weren't. Now that you're free and letting your little light shine, you appeal to him."

"My little light?"

"You know what I mean." Grace slanted a look at the mantle clock. "You said noon-ish. It's almost time for dinner."

"My connecting flight in New York was held up due to a non-working bathroom on the plane. The pilot came over the speaker and said they had to call Las Vegas to get a work order for a plumber to make repairs."

"Las Vegas?"

"A remote work order for a local plumber. We sat on the tarmac for over an hour. Once the guy got there, he had it fixed in a flash. I almost forgot about the small delay on the first leg of my flights. A maintenance crew left a screwdriver on the wing. I don't know what kind of trouble it would've caused if it had gone unnoticed."

"What you're trying not to say is that it could've gotten sucked into the engine."

Elaina stretched her mouth wide with a wince. "That went through my mind the entire time. Once we were in the air, the flight was smooth all the way to LaGuardia." Elaina slinked down onto the sofa and kicked off her shoes. "It's definitely been a wacky Wednesday and I'm glad we're due to have wine tonight."

"Maybe those strange incidents are a sign to keep your butt in Maine."

"You mean keep my butt away from Arden."

Grace pointed a finger gun at Elaina. "Yes. So much that." She closed the magazine she'd been paging through and lowered her voice to a whisper. "Why did the pointy-nose fish beckon you this time?"

At that precise moment, Tawny's door flung open and she raced into the living room. The slap of flip-flop type slippers on the stairs alerted them that Steph was on her way as well.

"Crap. I wanted to get the low-down ahead of those two."

Elaina looked around. "I didn't see a van in the driveway or parked out at the road. Elizabeth and Linus haven't arrived?"

"Not yet." Grace smirked. "You piqued our curiosities about Linus and then left for Ohio. Quick, give me the 4-1-1 on him."

"You'll know soon enough."

Grace toed her in the shin "You have brat-tendencies."

"Yes I do."

Tawny perched next to Elaina, instead of farther down on the sofa. "Don't keep me in suspense. Loosen those lips."

Steph extended her arm out. "Can you wait? I have a hankering for a cup of green tea. Anyone else care for tea?"

"I was on a germy airplane. A cup of green tea would be a wise choice." Elaina started to get up and Tawny pushed her back down.

"Holding out seems to be your specialty. No talky? No tea."

"Steph, have a seat before this one implodes." Once Steph settled in, Elaina began. "First of all, I want to apologize for making you worry and for postponing the scoop. It's just that some things shouldn't be sent via text message. I could've called, but I wasn't ready. I had certain emotions to wrestle."

"Arden's dad was gravely ill a while back. Did he...?"

"No, Steph. He's still very much alive. This wasn't about his father, it's about Rachel." Unshed tears for their sweet friend and for Arden burned the back of her eyes. "She's having issues with her pregnancy. Arden is scared out of his wits that she's going to lose the baby."

"Oh no!" Erupted from Grace.

The fear on Grace's face prompted Elaina to ease her panic. "I know where your thoughts went, Grace. Don't go there, okay? Isabella and the baby are fine. Rachel, on the other hand, has a weakened cervix. Arden called it cervical insufficiency. She could go into premature labor. They can't take that chance and she's been put on bed rest for the remaining months."

Grace gasped.

"Stop all ready." Elaina backpedaled right away. "You know what? It's a normal reaction. Women are worriers. It's what we do. Since you haven't seen Isabella's baby bump close up or felt the little one kick, you probably fret more than we can imagine. Maybe it's time for you to take a trip to Italy."

"WE should take a trip. I can't fly alone. What if the airplane's bathroom made me miss a connecting flight? I'd totally lose it if I saw a screwdriver on the wing."

In unison, Tawny and Steph said, "Huh?"

"Those are stories for later, over a glass of wine," Elaina suggested.

Grace tapped the arm of the recliner. "I don't get the

correlation between Arden needing you in Dayton and Rachel's cervix."

Tawny tried to hold in a laugh and jiggled the sofa in the process. Elaina gave her a pointed look.

"Sorry. I wasn't laughing at the situation. When it comes to your ex, all kinds of ridiculous thoughts pop into my head. I pictured him wanting you to... Never mind." Tawny motioned for Elaina to continue.

Elaina determined in that instant she would protect the degree of Arden's anguish. His tears were personal and they'd remain that way. "Arden tries to control everything. The one thing he really wants to have power over is out of his hands, and he feels like he's letting Rachel down."

Steph's eyes widened. "He said that?"

"Not in those exact words."

Stony loped into the living room and dropped down in front of Elaina. "I missed you too, boy. Where's the little pipsqueak?" A second later, Bailey ran in and lay beside Stony.

"Those short legs put you behind every time. Don't they, Bailey?" Tawny played with the velvet of Stony's ears. She did the same to Bailey. "Did he allow you to pop in to see Rachel while you were there?"

"Arden wouldn't have forbidden it. At the same time, he didn't want her to know he sent for me."

Tawny called Arden a wuss.

Elaina wouldn't defend Arden or her actions regarding him. "Here's the big picture. Even with all we've gone through, he still considers me a friend and wanted to talk."

"You can't go running every time his world tilts."

There were times Elaina wanted to put Tawny in a sleeper hold. This was one of those times. "You'd do it for Grady."

"Grady isn't a powerhouse like Arden. His influence only goes so far."

What Tawny didn't articulate struck Elaina more than what she said. Instead of unyielding opposition, she'd left room for maybe. "You wouldn't zip to Ohio to aid Grady?"

"Nope."

Elaina snickered. "Stronger women than you have had to retract their lexis."

"Retract their lexis? Speak English, woman."

"It means eat their words."

Tawny rolled her eyes. "I don't foresee eating anything, except Steph's carrot salad. I turned my nose up initially, but one taste and I was hooked. She used olive oil, cayenne pepper, garlic, cumin, and… What else did you put in it, Steph?"

"Wine vinegar and cilantro. Tawny, you can list the ingredients to all my recipes as a way to distract us. When you're done, it won't change the fact Grady still has a piece of your heart. If he called right now and asked you to come to Ohio, you'd trip over yourself to get out the door."

A sheepish grin tipped Tawny's mouth. "That is not true." She uncoiled from the comfort of the couch. "I'm not waiting until nine o'clock to have a glass of wine."

Grace, Steph, and Elaina exchanged knowing looks.

"Forget tea, I'm getting wine too." Steph took off after Tawny.

Elaina asked, "Am I missing something?"

"Hard to tell with her."

Elaina sifted through her current thoughts regarding Tawny. "She's too adamant about what I shouldn't do. And she can go from clowning around to tears in a blink."

"We've blamed her boys for stressing her out due to their lack of communication. They're to blame for some of the swift changes in her mood, but I think something else is at play here." Grace tapped her head.

"Things we store up there eventually come out. We have to give Tawny space to work through whatever it might be, or to gradually leak it to us."

"No wonder Arden can't let go."

"I'm not sure what you mean, Grace."

"Well then, I'll lay it out for you. You support us when we ask, and even when we don't. You keep a level head and try to understand our madness. You, my friend, have an extraordinary gift."

Elaina objected to the analysis with a scoff.

"And you're extremely humble."

"We all bring something special to the table."

A smile covered Grace's entire face. "I want to bring a glass of wine to the table."

"Me too."

Almost to the kitchen to join Tawny and Steph, the doorbell stopped them in their tracks. They looked at each other and said, "Linus."

Grace hurried ahead of Elaina and smashed her eye

against the peek-hole in the door. "I don't see him."

"I'm sure he came. Brace yourself. You're going to fall head over heels for him."

A playful grin crimped the corners of Grace's mouth. "I'm in love with Philip."

Grace was going to be surprised when she discovered Linus had four legs and was possibly the size of three dogs; although, Elizabeth didn't come right out and say he was a large breed, she'd alluded to it, and had bought a van just for him. He could very well be a Saint Bernard or a Great Dane.

Grace eased open the door. "Welcome to the Four Sassy Chicks Bed and Breakfast. I'm Grace – the least sassy of the bunch." She stretched to look past Elizabeth. "Is Linus parking your vehicle?"

A look of confusion crossed Elizabeth's face. "He's not old enough to drive."

"But I thought...."

Elaina told Elizabeth to come in.

The second Elizabeth stepped into the foyer, Stony yowled and Bailey went into a barking frenzy.

A small yip came from somewhere close.

Elizabeth opened her over-sized purse, and a tiny head peered out.

Sweet mother of assumption! Elaina couldn't have been more wrong about Linus. There was nothing large about him. He was one of the tiniest dogs on the planet – a miniature Chihuahua that could fit in the palm of her hand and in any purse.

"Meet Linus."

"Be still my heart." Grace spoke baby talk to the little dog. "You're a cutie. Yes you are." Reaching for him was a mistake. Linus established boundaries with a low growl.

"That's what I wanted to be upfront with you about, Elaina. Linus is a protector with no fear regarding the size of his adversary. Should someone try to harm me, he'll bite the enemy until his teeth fall out or he collapses from over-exertion; whichever comes first."

Tawny wandered up and shook her head at Grace. "I'd growl too if someone spoke to me like I'm a baby." She started to jut a hand out to Elizabeth, but pulled it back when Linus stretched up. "I'm Tawny, and this is my boy, Stony." Stony brushed against her leg. "He's also protective; you just can't tell right away."

"Ahh. He takes a more subtle approach. Bite first? Ask questions later?"

Tawny snickered. "Someone would really have to get up in my grill. Then he'd be all over them."

Grace picked up Bailey. "Don't kid yourself, Tawn'. Dogs have a keen sense about people. If he thought you were in danger – or any of us for that matter – he'd bare his teeth and go after the perp."

"You have a thing for cops. Now you're starting to talk like one."

"No. I have a thing for Philip. Elaina's the one who loves cops."

Elaina lifted an eyebrow.

"I've just been told, ever-so- delicately, to shut my yapper."

"I'm starting to understand the name of your business."

Elaina chuckled. "It truly defines us. Let's get you situated."

"That would be great. My boy's worn out."

Linus looked fine. Elizabeth, on the other hand, had clear signs of exhaustion with dark under-eye circles. "We were about to have a glass of wine. Would you care to join us?"

"Thank you for the offer, but I think I'll pass. This little cuddle-bug and I are going to unwind after the long drive."

Portland was just shy of being a four-hour drive from New Haven, Connecticut.

Elizabeth must've tuned into Elaina's thought. "We lingered in Connecticut too long, but I had to start my day with a bagel topped with lox, cream cheese, cucumber, and capers."

Tawny made a face. "What's lox?"

Steph piped up with an answer. "Brined salmon. Yum."

Elizabeth smiled at Steph. "Not everyone's familiar with the term."

"Steph's a foodie. She knows about weird food," Grace explained.

Elizabeth's weariness appeared to vanish on the spot. "Same here. Some people eat to live, I live to eat. I'm all about pleasing my palate. In fact, Linus and I walked around the campus of Yale University for a few hours after breakfast, so I could eat lunch at one of my favorite restaurants. Since I'm going to be gone for a few months, I just had to have an order of fried pickle chips and corn fritters made with bacon, cherry peppers, corn, and green onions. Linus is a foodie too. The places where I eat have gotten to know Linus and spoil him with treats." She looked at her watch. "It's time to feed my boy. I'm feeling especially peckish too. Can you suggest a restaurant that makes unusual and incredible food – and one who delivers?"

Grace put Steph on the hot seat. "You could make Elizabeth something strange yet scrumptious."

Elizabeth steadfastly declined the offer. "You're a bed and breakfast, not a bed and dinner service. I'm looking forward to what you'll serve in the morning. For now, Linus and I are going to get into our PJ's and watch our favorite shows, while sampling local takeout."

"He has pajamas?"

"There's not much to him. I have to keep my little man warm."

Nick arrived home and entered through the back door like a herd of elephants stampeding the Serengeti. He hollered a boisterous hello.

Linus jerked at the noise and ducked down in Elizabeth's purse. "Let the pajama party begin."

Elaina said it was time to show them to their room.

"I should inform you that Linus is prone to barking frenzies. It's the oddest thing. All of the sudden he breaks into a yipping episode, for no apparent reason. He has weak vocal chords, so the noise shouldn't disturb you or your other guests."

"I can't make that claim about Stony or Bailey. They bark for a reason, usually when one gets the upper hand.

Actually, Stony has more of a yowl. Bailey, like Linus, doesn't have a strong set of pipes, yet she lets you know she's around."

Elizabeth opened her purse wider to speak to Linus. "We chose the right place."

* * *

Steph smacked her lips after imbibing in a sip of Sangria. "Mighty tasty."

Elaina popped the cork on a new bottle of blackberry wine.

Tawny filled an over-sized goblet with dry red.

Grace splashed white merlot into the nearest drinking vessel – a coffee cup. She raised it in the air. "These are the exact adult beverages we had the day we met." A smile touched her lips. "I never thought wine would have such a profound effect on my life."

"The wine played a small part." Elaina did a round of glass clinking. "I never expected to be this happy. Thank you, ladies."

"Aww!" Steph gave her a hug. "I never knew friendship could be so powerful. I draw strength from each of you every day."

Tawny chugged half her wine. "I've learned over the past several months to never say never."

Elaina noted an unusual gleam in Tawny's milk chocolate eyes. Tawny caught her staring and looked away.

"I'm tucking away all this sappy love stuff," Grace said

with a satisfied smile, "to announce that I mulled over Elaina's suggestion, and I've decided to fly to Italy to feel the baby kick. I'm the grandma, and I want to be part of Isabella's pregnancy."

Tawny spontaneously said she couldn't go along, although she didn't offer a reason.

Steph made clear that it wasn't a good time for her to leave Maine because she and Nick wanted to finish the cookbook as soon as possible.

Grace tapped Elaina's shoulder. "I know you can't go. The reservations are piling up. I spazzed out earlier when you told me what took place in Dayton and New York. Now that I've had a few minutes to think things through, I realize those were just minor inconveniences."

Elaina grinned. "I can read between the lines. You're going to make Philip go along."

"Yep."

"Grace, it should be easy to talk him into going. Mention the statue of David by Michelangelo. Or Leonardo Da Vinci's Last Supper and the Mona Lisa. Philip will have his bags packed before you ask if he has a passport."

"You're one clever chick, Samuels. I wouldn't have thought about the art angle."

"There's also the romance angle to consider." Steph smiled over the rim of her wine glass. "Tell Philly-boy the two of you can drift down the canals of Venice while a gondolier serenades you."

"Yeah, that'll make him want to go. Not."

Their short bursts of laughter were interrupted by a ping from Tawny's cell phone. Tawny grabbed the phone from the counter and shoved it in the back pocket of her jeans without reading the message.

Chapter Eight

- Love doesn't always make sense! -

At precisely midnight, Linus exercised his little lungs with nonstop yipping. Elizabeth had claimed the miniature dog couldn't project a real bark. Over time, she must've gotten used to the noise not realizing he could reach a certain decibel.

Elaina checked on Stony and Bailey, who were curled up together near the purple beast. Any second, Linus would wake them and they'd join in the chorus. To her surprise, neither one stirred.

Giving the kitchen one last inspection to make sure the stove was turned off and the back door was locked, Elaina yawned and flicked off the light above the sink. The house was in total darkness, except for the nightlights plugged into the walls. She noticed a tiny slice of illumination coming out from under Tawny's bedroom door.

Tawny inched opened the door, just enough to step out of her room without being seen.

Elaina didn't move a muscle or breathe. She watched Tawny's clandestine movements. This verified what her gut knew all along – something was up with her dear, good friend.

Dressed in a hoodie and rubber boots, Tawny crept to the sunroom. The automatic sensor light turned on and then went off right away – indicating Tawny had hit the switch to deactivate it. She did the same thing to the light on the wrap-around porch. Had she done it out of courtesy for Elizabeth? Or remain on the sly?

"You seriously make me wonder some days, Tawn'. Tonight I'm too tired to let my curiosity get the best of me." Almost to the basement, Elaina flinched when another door opened. This time it was Elizabeth's.

Elizabeth gasped at the presence of another person. "I didn't mean to frighten you."

"You're fine. I was heading to bed."

"I guess meeting someone in the semi-darkness is a hazard of staying in a bed and breakfast versus a hotel. In a hotel, people are always moving about, regardless of the hour. Here it's extremely quiet and I assumed everyone was already asleep." Elizabeth held Linus in the crook of her arm. "My boy has a small bladder, which means we'll make frequent trips outside during the night."

That explained the dark shadows under Elizabeth's eyes.

"I may sleep in, if that's okay."

"We don't follow a strict breakfast schedule unless we have a lot of guests. Then the kitchen is open between seven and ten. Since it's just you and your sweet pup, you can stumble out whenever you're ready, and we'll whip something up."

"Thank you for accommodating us."

"We're happy to have you. The closest exit is through the sunroom. I should make you aware that Tawny just stepped outside so you won't be startled a second time. You know what? I'll join you."

Together they made their way to the porch. They found Tawny sitting on the steps with her phone glued to her ear.

Tawny's eyes rounded with surprise. She sprang to her feet and ended the call. "Why are you…? Oh. Linus has to do his business." She talked fast, making it difficult to get a word in. "I had to take care of business too – mine involved family. I came outside so I wouldn't disturb you."

Elizabeth apologized. "We didn't mean to intrude."

"No. No. You're fine. When our babies have to go, it doesn't matter if it's midnight or noon. They let us know and we're on it."

Tawny's skulking around now made sense. She was catching up with one of her sons; either Bo in California or Quentin in Oregon – midnight in Maine, nine o'clock on the west coast. Elaina expelled a lengthy yawn. "It's mattress time. Do either of you need anything before I tuck in?"

Tawny said a quick, "No."

"I'm good too, but thanks." Elizabeth put Linus down, and he scampered to a nearby oak tree.

In the brightness cast from the porch light, the same

peculiar glitter from earlier shone in Tawny's eyes and something unsettling spiked into Elaina's thoughts. Tawny might've made contact with someone from that dating site, and she wasn't ready to let them know. *Be careful, Tawn'.*

* * *

Steph and Nick had scooted out the door early to get things started at the restaurant. Instead of catching a few extra winks on her day off, Tawny had gotten up early. She'd wolfed down a bowl of cereal and headed to the mall to buy new scrubs. Grace and Philip had filled their travel mugs with coffee and were on their way to an antique store in Bar Harbor that advertised Victorian door knockers.

Elaina made a fresh pot of coffee in case Elizabeth woke sooner than she'd anticipated, and then left a note on the table stating she was taking the dogs out for an early morning stroll. Shoving her phone and a ten dollar bill into her pocket, she led the dogs outside just as the grey cloud that had hung heavily in the sky since daybreak disappeared. Elaina inhaled several times to fill her lungs with fresh air and exhaled with a smile.

Mid-April in Portland was unusually warm, at least according to the local TV weather team. They predicted it would remain that way for most of the month. The remnants of winter were ebbing and crocuses started to push through the ground. A flock of Herring gulls squawked and patrolled the shoreline. Maine in the spring was indeed something to behold.

Instead of their usual route, Elaina tugged the pooches down Fore Street and made a right onto Union. They walked until they came to Commercial Street. She checked the addresses on the buildings, knowing the coffee house she'd seen in the Portland newspaper had to be close. According to their ad, they served fabulous maple lattes. Elaina's mouth watered at the thought of hot coffee with maple syrup and just the right amount of vanilla, topped with whipped cream and a sprinkle of cinnamon.

The oval sign announcing the shop came into view. "The place is pet-friendly. They might have a treat for you." Stony turned and stared. If he could speak, she'd say, "Huh?"

Stony's nose did double-time. He sniffed the air more than he usually did and then dropped his nose to the ground breathing in every inch of pavement like he was a police dog on an important case. He arched his back and barked at something straight ahead.

A familiar head of light brown hair and the olive-colored pea coat that hung daily in their closet filled Elaina's vision. She squinted to home in on Tawny and... Elaina couldn't believe her eyes. She squinted harder to make sure she wasn't seeing things. No, the guy wasn't an illusion. Tawny had her arms thrown around his neck and she was pressing into him like they were lovers.

Stony went from barking to yowling when he identified the scent as his owner.

Instinctively, Elaina pulled on the leashes, so she,

Stony and Bailey could duck into a nearby alley. Stony continued his happy yowl and resisted the hold Elaina had on him. "Not now, boy." She crouched to be eye to snout. "We have to let this play out. Maybe she'll tell us what's going on or maybe she won't. Time will tell." Elaina planted a kiss on his nose and ran a hand over the length of Bailey. "Good thing neither of you can spill the beans on Tawn'. I'll have difficulty keeping this to myself, but I will." She stood. "No maple latte today. We'd better head home and see if Elizabeth and Linus are awake."

The mention of Linus twitched Stony's ears.

Elaina was tempted to take another look. She coaxed herself not to, by repeating a few times, "Leave it alone." Portland was a decent size city. There should've been a zero chance of stumbling upon Tawny being touchy, feely with.... "Tawn', I hope you know what you're doing."

* * *

Out of breath from being dragged by Stony, Elaina juggled Bailey in her arms and tried to answer her cell phone at the same time. "Hey, Steph, what's up?"

"You sound like you need oxygen."

"That's because I do."

Steph snorted a laugh. "I really should stick around longer in the mornings to see what goes on."

"Stony took off at breakneck speed when he saw a squirrel run up a tree. I had to scoop up Bailey to keep from trampling her with my size sevens." Elaina could hear Steph repeating everything she said word for word to Nick.

Nick snatched Steph's phone. "You can't buy that kind of entertainment."

Elaina got Stony and her breathing under control at the same time. "I'm sure there's funny stuff that goes on in the restaurant to cause a few laughs too."

"Nah. Everything runs efficiently here. No. Wait. Steph just skidded on a chunk of potato."

The noise of a loud whack reached Elaina's ears, followed by an, "Oww!"

"Sometimes you just have to backhand phone stealers." Steph spoke to Elaina, but also to Nick. "Yeah, that'll teach you." She giggled. "Still there?"

"Taking it all in. For a second, I thought you wiped out against a refrigerator or doorway."

"He caught me before I crashed."

"Your knight in shining armor?"

"Heck no. He's the one who dropped the potato."

Stony tried to scale the tree in front of the bed and breakfast.

"Give it up, boy. The squirrel is laughing at you from the top branch."

"Question. Are Elizabeth and Linus still there? Or did they take off for already?"

"I haven't fed them breakfast." Elaina looked at her watch. "I need to get to it. Why'd you call?"

"The potato-dropper wanted me to ask if we could all get together for dinner tonight at the restaurant."

"Does he need a few guinea pigs to try a new recipe?"

"I heard that, Samuels."

"Stop eavesdropping, Nicholas. Steph, do you have me on speaker?"

"My bad. I was talking and chopping celery."

"Nick wants to feed us steak and lobster tonight, right?" Elaina teased, to get a rise out of Nick.

"As a matter of fact, I do."

"Do you have to use them up before they go bad?"

Nick roared with a hearty laugh. "Be nice or I'll put laxative in your dessert."

"That would not be good. I'll quit sassing, mostly because I have eggs and pancakes to make. Hold on a sec." Elaina opened the backyard gate and unsnapped the dog leashes so Stony and Bailey could run off some excess energy. "I'm back. Tell me about tonight in five words or less."

"Be here or else."

"Four words. I'm impressed. It doesn't really tell me anything, but okay. I can definitely make it. I'm not sure about the others." Elaina thought specifically about Tawny. "I may have to eat their lobsters."

The humor left Nick's voice. "I'd really like for everyone to show up."

Another squirrel decided to taunt Stony. The rodent scampered around the base of a birch tree and then did a spectacular hop onto a maple tree. Those little claws dug in and within seconds the bushy-tailed animal ascended out of Stony's reach. "And I'd like for Stony to come to grips with the fact he's never going to catch a squirrel."

"He's doing what dogs do."

"He's a pain."

"No he's not. You love that dog like he's your child. You baby him. Correction – you love and baby them both."

"Maybe. Maybe not. I'm going inside to make eggs. Honestly, Nick, there's a small chance I may not make it to dinner. Elizabeth and Linus may want to stay on."

Elaina could hear a muffled conversation. Suddenly Nick was gone and Steph was back.

"Nick says to bring Elizabeth along."

"She can't leave Linus in a strange place."

Steph shared Elaina's concern. "He says to sneak Linus in the back door. We'll keep the Health Department out of the loop."

Interesting. The one thing you could count on besides incredible food at Nick's restaurant was cleanliness – well, when he wasn't dropping potatoes in the kitchen. Nick grudging allowed service animals, but according to Steph, he didn't take his eyes off them for a second. For him to allow Linus in, meant something big was about to go down. Did Nick, II, buy that winery outside Portland? Was tonight's dinner to celebrate his son branching out? "I'll be there one way or the other. Send a text to the rest of the gang. I'd do it, but I'm maxed out handling squirrel-hunters and scrambling eggs are about to happen."

"I'll send a text as soon as we're done talking. Can you delay making breakfast for another couple minutes?" Steph's tone had changed from lighthearted to serious.

"What's on your mind?"

Stony took off after a leaf blowing in the wind.

"Steph, talk fast. The clock is ticking."

"Are you getting a strange vibe from Tawny?"

So, she and Grace weren't the only ones who noticed. Elaina was thankful Elizabeth looked through the glass of the back door.

"I can't go into it right now, Steph. Elizabeth and Linus want my attention."

"Is that a sneaky way of saying you DID notice, but you don't want to start trouble by agreeing?"

* * *

"I didn't mean to keep you waiting."

"You didn't. Linus and I are still wiping the sleep from our eyes. I read your note and thought you might allow him to run with your dogs for a few minutes."

"Stony and Bailey would love to play with him."

Dressed in a granny nightgown, boots, and a zip-up cardigan, Elizabeth stepped out on the patio with the tiny pooch.

Elaina put her hands out to take Linus. Ensconced in a green knitted sweater appliquéd with dog bones, Linus blinked up at her. "Look at you all cozy and warm in that sweater. You're a trend-setter, sweet pup. Stony and Bailey are going to be jealous."

Elizabeth lowered her head, but looked up through her lashes as if embarrassed. "I have a suitcase filled with clothes for him. My friends think I go overboard. How can I not? He's my one true love."

"I totally get it." The mention of one true love caused Elaina's brain to conjure up a vision of Jess. Maybe if she'd knitted him sweaters… *Stop*. He didn't deserve space in her head. "I just talked to Steph and Nick. In the conversation, Nick said the same thing about me. According to him, I love these dogs like they're my kids. He's right, I do." She glanced back at the dogs. Bailey was trying and failing to jump high enough to get Stony's tail. "They give love easily." She put Linus down and instructed Stony and Bailey to be nice.

Stony sniffed Linus. He established his role as the alpha by placing a meaty paw on him.

"Stonyyyyy."

Stony released the miniature Chihuahua. Linus took off as fast as his small legs would take him. Stony and Bailey set chase.

Elizabeth broke into a giggle when Linus tried to evade the bigger dogs by hiding behind an Elm tree. He stuck his head out to locate Stony and Bailey.

Stony looked back at Elaina.

"Buddy-up to him, Stone-man. Show him around."

Linus reared his head again and took off running toward the gazebo. He stopped abruptly and went down on his belly.

"He gets winded, but recovers fast."

Sure enough, he jumped up and bared his teeth at Stony before making another mad dash to the gazebo. A game of canine hide-and-seek began. Linus was small enough to slip through the slats. Stony and Bailey tried to tag team the hundred-mile-an-hour pooch, to no avail. Linus was there one second, gone the next.

"I could watch them for hours, although it would impede us getting to Calais to visit my cousin, Bridgette. Bridge' has always stopped at my place on her way to Maryland to see her niece. I promised her that once I retired, I'd come to Calais. She says I'll fall in love with the area." Elizabeth rubbed her hands together. "Teaching was my thing for years, now it's traveling. I'm also into collecting rocks. I plan to pick one up at every stop." She grinned. "I admit to taking a small polished stone from your landscape."

"You can have as many as you like."

"Thank you. Bridge' says I love weird stuff, yet she smothers a raccoon named Arthur with affection."

Elaina lifted her shoulders in a shrug. "Love doesn't always make sense. Sometimes we find it with people, sometimes with a raccoon."

* * *

Nicholas parked himself at the end of the table and clapped to get everyone's attention. "Steph and I are glad to see everyone. With tourist season knocking at our doors, this may be the last opportunity we have to be together for a while."

"I agree. Things are already getting crazy." Philip raised his eyebrows. "I have people wanting to schedule private showings with wine and cheese at my art studio." He winked at Grace. "Our art studio."

"We don't have everything ready. Over the next few

weeks, we'll have to pour all our time and energy into getting it finished." Grace made eye contact with Elaina.

Elaina took Grace's stare as her way of asking to opt out of bed and breakfast duties. She consented with a smile.

Tawny was unusually quiet.

Philip grabbed the basket of French bread and proceeded to slather a slice with apple butter. "Bring on the real food, I'm starving."

Nick, II, and his wife, Margaret sat near Nicholas and Grace. They were huddled close like newlyweds should be. Nick, II, stopped embracing and whispering to his wife long enough to address Philip's comment. "We heard your belly growl clear down here." He snorted a laugh and Margaret's cheeks dimpled with a coy smile.

"Appetizers are on their way, I promise. First, I have something important to take care of." He beamed a ray of happiness at Steph. You could hear his joy when he spoke. "Steph, you and I clicked from the moment we laid eyes on one another. I don't believe fate played a part in putting us together. I think you were meant for me all along. We like the same things and finish each other's sentences. We're an old married couple, without the rings and certificate. We're also best friends. Even though we haven't known each other a full year," he took her hand, "it feels like I've known you forever. Waking up beside you every morning is incredible, but I don't want to continue cohabitating with you without giving you a commitment. I asked your dad and my son for their permission." He got down on one knee.

Sharp intakes of air reverberated around the private dining room, but the loudest came from Steph. She put a hand on her heart. "You talked to my dad?" In the same breath, she thanked Nick, II.

Philip saluted. "Way to go, Nick."

Grace shushed him.

"I love you, Stephanie Mathews. When we were in California, I was restless and couldn't figure out why. My son hit the nail on the head. He said it was because I hadn't seen you for twenty-four hours. He was right." Nicholas smiled warmly at his son. "Nick suggested we make a pit stop in Ohio on the way home from our trip. Your parents are great, sweetheart. They're overjoyed that their daughter has found true love. And they approve of the man you chose to love – me."

Nick and Margaret gave him the thumbs-up.

"Call me a sap, but I look forward to your smile, your scent, your voice, and some things I can't say with everyone listening. It boils down to you and me forevermore. I love you more than I could ever express, Steph. Would you do me the honor of becoming my wife?"

Happy tears flowed unrestrained from Steph's eyes. "I love you too, Nicholas Augustine." A huge smile accompanied the tears. "You want to marry me!" To everyone else, she said, "He wants to marry me!" Relocating the hand that had been on her heart to Nicholas's, she gave him a boisterous, "Yes! I'd love to be your other half."

Nick pulled her up and tightly against him. "My best half."

"Congratulations," bounced around the room. Hugs and handshakes took up the next ten minutes. Finally, Nick, II, summoned the wait staff. A cart was wheeled in with bottles of champagne and appetizers.

"Before we pop the corks on the bubbly, I have something to give you, Steph."

"You picked out a ring? Elaina did you give him my ring size?"

"Nope."

"It's not a ring. Tomorrow we'll pick one out together." Nick removed an envelope he'd kept hidden under the tablecloth and gave it to Steph.

"What's this?"

Nick pressed his lips to her hand. "You'll see."

Steph roamed her gaze over Nicholas and she did the same thing to the others, as though needing them to calm her nerves. They each shored her up with a nod.

Grace prompted her to open the envelope so they'd all know what was inside.

Steph slid a fingernail under the sealed flap and gingerly tore the envelope. Straightening the document, she began to read quietly. You couldn't hear the words. As each second ticked off, her eyes grew a little bigger until the green sparkle could've easily been seen by NASA's satellites. "Nick?"

Nick put an arm around her.

Tawny, always handy with the snark, asked if it was a pre-nup.

Nick and Steph spoke a few quiet words to each other. They parted just enough to allow Nick to fish a handkerchief from his pocket. He gently blotted tears from Steph's cheeks. "What do you think?"

"I've never had anyone love me this much." Steph did a half turn. "Not to say all of you don't love me as much as Nick does."

Elaina said what she was feeling. "Our love for you is more than you can imagine, Steph, but it's different from Nick's."

Steph took the handkerchief and blew her nose.

Philip couldn't wait any longer. "I'm dying to know what's on the paper."

Steph and Nick continued to smile at one another. "He bought us a home. It's a block down the street from the bed and breakfast – the house with the rusty ship's anchor in the front yard."

"I love that place. It has a widow's walk perched on top. The double-front door is modern, but it with classic appeal. Someone did their homework to keep it line or at least make it look like it's from the same era the house was built. Something old made new." Tawny's brows crinkled for no more than a breath.

Elaina noticed Tawny's reaction and was aware of the motive.

Steph clung to Nick, as if she feared it was all a dream.

Nick laid his forehead on Steph's. "I wanted you to be close to your..." He paused to correct his thought. "I wanted us to be close to our friends."

"That is so great, Nick." Steph stepped on her tiptoes and thanked him with a swift kiss.

"Another selling point was the loft apartment above

the extra garage in the back of the property."

Tawny asked why that was a selling point.

Instead of answering directly, Nicholas whispered something to his Steph.

"A thousand times yes, Nick. Do you mind if I ask them?"

Nicholas swept his hand toward his son and daughter-in-law.

"Nick and Margaret, instead of continuing to rent the apartment you're currently in, what do you think about moving above the garage? It would help you save money to buy your own place some day and also help you stash money away for the down payment on a winery, if you still plan to buy one."

"We wouldn't be intruding?"

Steph waved away the notion. "We're family, or soon will be. Your dad and I want you around."

Philip teased, "There goes the neighborhood."

Tawny mentioned that the occupants of the bed and breakfast were slowly decreasing.

Nick assured Tawny that he and Steph wouldn't walk away from the business. "We're fully committed to the success of the Four Sassy Chicks. Though things could occasionally get tricky due to the book tour, you know."

"And the cooking show that will come from the book tour," Elaina added.

"Yes, and that," Steph said with a smile. "Please know that I will always be one of the sassy chicks. I have the tats to prove it." She lifted her ankle to show the infinity tattoo and then pulled at the neckline of her blouse to reveal the one written in script lettering – *One of Four Sassy Chicks.*

Nick, II, popped the cork on a bottle of champagne. "It's time to celebrate with these lovebirds." He poured Elaina a glass and asked her to make the first toast.

Elaina wet her lips with the effervescent wine and raised her glass. "To Nick and Steph—your quirky personalities, kind hearts, and energy have added so much to our lives. We love you and wish you years of joy and success."

Tawny pushed out of her chair and held her glass high. "Elaina summed up what we all feel, so I'll keep this short. Nick and Steph, this is such a romantic moment. Thank you for allowing us to be a part of it." She blew them a kiss and encouraged Nick, II, to go next.

"Dad, I haven't seen you this happy in a long time. You're a great father and role model. Steph is truly the one for you. Steph, you're a sweetheart. Your selflessness and ambition astounds me at every turn. Together you'll do great things. One of those things is showing Margaret and me how love is supposed to go. You're not even married yet, but you work side by side, always looking out for one another. We adore you!"

The others took turns expressing their sentiments.

Food arrived and dining commenced.

When the waiters brought cheesecake for dessert, Tawny clanged her champagne flute with her fork. "Steph and Nick, tonight belongs exclusively to you. But if I could steal five minutes of your spotlight, I'd be forever in your debt."

The room went from lively conversation to complete quiet in a heartbeat.

"Take all the time you need." Steph slid a look at Elaina.

"Thank you." Tawny grabbed her glass and guzzled champagne. With all eyes upon her, she began. "Tonight was about showing no fear when it comes to love." She wrung her hands and almost knocked over her water glass. She lowered her eyes to the tablecloth for an excessive amount of time.

Grace threw out a guess to restart the conversation. "Did you meet someone?"

Tawny's head shot up. "No! Well, sort of."

"How do you sort of meet someone?"

The stretchy fabric of Tawny's shirt must've felt like it swelled on her body. She pulled at the neckline and tugged the material out from under her armpits. Another big hint that she was a mass of nerves, she moved around in her chair like she was polishing it with her bottom. The rooms' soft lighting hit her face just right, making the beads of sweat that had collected above her lip glisten. "I, uh..." She muttered something no one could make out.

"Say again," Grace urged.

Elaina knew exactly what Tawny was about to reveal. She wanted to shore her up with a hug first, but it might make Tawny clam up.

Tawny grabbed her glass of champagne again, and chugged the remaining bubbly.

"Out with it," Steph gently encouraged. "We're friends. You can tell us anything."

Wiping her mouth with the back of her hand, Tawny blurted, "I'm in a relationship." She looked directly at Elaina. "With Grady."

Chapter Nine

~ Even when it's awkward, it's all good! ~

Tawny had given clues with her twitchy behavior and the 'something old made new' remark. Elaina hadn't needed them, but she wouldn't let on that she was already privy to her and Grady hooking back up. She was glad Tawny had bared her soul, because toting around that secret would've grown increasingly difficult.

"I really didn't want to take this cheesecake home. Nick wouldn't take no for an answer. He said to share it with Grady." Tawny stashed it on the floor in the back of the SUV so it wouldn't slide around and then climbed into the front passenger seat. She dropped her head back and closed her eyes.

Elaina didn't start the engine. She closed her eyes too and relaxed her shoulders with a quiet sigh. "Never in a million years did I imagine you and Grady getting back together."

"That makes two of us."

Simultaneously they opened their eyes and looked at each other.

"For the longest time, I didn't hear from him, and truthfully, I would've thrown up if I had. Several weeks ago, he texted me in the middle of the night, telling me he was sorry for being an ass all those years. We've been sending messages back and forth ever since. In fact, when I went to the restroom earlier in the restaurant, it was to answer one of his texts. Grady said he realized how he'd tried to squeeze me into an unrealistic mold, knowing full-well no one was perfect. He admitted he was the one who needed to improve, not me."

Elaina pondered the sensitive disclosure. "He obviously hasn't stopped thinking about your time together and wants to correct the stuff he got wrong. That's big, Tawn'."

"Grady's discovered a lot about us and himself. Thanks to a wonderful psychologist named Bernie."

"He sought help?"

"He did. The fact he's taking responsibility for everything that caused us to split, makes me want to cry." Tawny fanned her face. "I can't let him shoulder all the blame. I was no angel."

"It's hard to remain angelic when your spouse is being a pain."

"I've said this before, but it's worth repeating – I wish I'd known you sooner, Elaina. Instead of teetering on that ledge for years, you would've talked me down from it and things might've turned out differently."

"We weren't supposed to meet until we did. It was part of a specific plan laid out for us."

"What plan?"

"I think we get a detailed schematic the moment we take our first breath." Elaina thought about her viewpoint. It could be perceived as out-there, but she believed it wholeheartedly. "Included in the plan is a hard-to-decipher treasure map, complete with mazes, walls to scale, hints that I swear are written in Chinese, and other carefully designed obstacles meant to throw us off course and test our resilience. Some people get to the big X and do a victory dance when they find the treasure; most of us never make it through the maze."

"You're such a visual person. You probably have charts and graphs in your head too."

"There aren't any charts and graphs." Elaina stretched her neck from side to side, trying to work out a kink. "Grady's stirred some powerful feelings in you, hasn't he?"

Tawny sighed.

"I'm sensing you want me to tell you to go for it. You'd also like for me to give you a good shake and advise you to do the opposite."

"You're spot-on. The wise ninety-nine percent of me knows it would behoove me to sidestep the sleeping dog. The daring and foolish one percent thinks I should at least poke it."

"What's your heart telling you?"

"That Grady's sincere and things will be better this time around."

"So it's actually going to happen. You're going to date your ex-husband."

"That sounds dreadful."

Elaina smoothed a hand up and down Tawny's arm. "It's not dreadful. It's exciting. You and Grady have a second chance at love."

To Elaina's shock, Tawny's voice quivered and the vault of her tightly guarded secrets opened. "He wasn't always a total jerk. He knew how to make my body sing. Yeah, I know, that's TMI, but I want my ears to hear it too, so I know I'm doing the right thing. Grady had skills like you wouldn't believe. When we first got married, we made love in every room and on the porch. Sometimes on the way home from a night out, we'd park the car along the road and steam up the windows."

The urge to say, "Shh," or to don a pair of noise-cancelling headphones was strong. Intimate details of a person's love life should be cherished, not shared, but if it helped Tawny figure things out, then Elaina would listen.

"He bought me flowers and sexy lingerie. After we had Bo, the dynamics of our private time changed."

"I'm sure that happens in every marriage. Those carefree days of sex on the porch are replaced with feeding the baby at two o'clock in the morning, rocking the little one back to sleep, and trying to get some shut-eye yourself before the alarm goes off."

"Grady seemed turned off by the changes in my body after two pregnancies. He didn't come right out and say it, but his lack of interest said it for him. As if that wasn't enough, he criticized every little thing I did or didn't do."

"Did you talk to him about it?"

"About being critical? Yes, absolutely. Regarding his lack of physical interest, that's where the I'm-no-angel-confession comes in. Instead of airing my concerns for him to confirm or deny, I held onto them. Needless to say, it caused us to grow apart." Tawny expelled a heavy breath. "Today I held nothing back. I brought up my stretch marks and the size of my boobs, which doubled after I had Quentin. Grady said without those stretch marks he'd never have two awesome sons. And he considers my boobs to be my second best feature. He said my chest is fantastic." The quivery emotion in Tawny's voice ebbed.

"I thought he was a leg man, and that's why he wanted you to wear stilettos all the time."

"Apparently he likes more than just my legs. I can't believe you remembered about the stilettos and funny you should mention them right now. They were part of my text-conversation with Grady tonight. I flat out told him I'm done with high heels. I made it known that they hurt my feet and caused spider veins."

"Heels can actually cause spider veins?"

"In one of my nursing journals, I read that the trend to wear extremely highly heels can impact how your calf muscles contract – or rather, not contract as much as they should. Less blood gets pushed out, and the venous blood pressure increases, which can stress the valves in your leg. I withheld the fact that crossing your legs can be the cause too."

"I don't always understand what you're talking about, but it's great when you get on a roll."

"I get carried away sometimes."

"You're passionate about what you do."

"I guess."

"Grady's okay with you shucking the heels?"

Tawny played with the clasp on her watch. "His psychologist told him the shoes were a control thing and he agreed."

"Kudos to the psychologist for helping Grady return to the man you once knew. By the way, if your chest ranks second, what does he consider your best feature?"

Tawny batted her eyelashes. "My eyes took first place."

"They are spectacular, you little minx."

Tawny pulled the seatbelt across her and latched it. "Do you think I'm making a mistake by letting Grady back in?"

"Only you can answer that."

"Would you take Arden back?"

Elaina drove out of the restaurant parking lot. "He's married."

They rode in silence during the five-minute drive back home. Elaina spent the time combing through all that Tawny had shared and she was sure Tawn' was going back over it as well.

Tawny juggled the cheesecake while toeing off her shoes. "Hypothetically, if Arden were available and no longer being a pain in your tookus, would consider rekindling your relationship?"

"The he's-married bit didn't satisfy that quirky little mind of yours?"

"It did not. And now that you've had time to let my question penetrate that amazing brain of yours, give me a better answer."

Elaina took two forks from the silverware drawer and opened the box containing the cheesecake. She drew an imaginary line. "Grady can have that half. You and I are going to polish off this half." Forking a smidgen of cheesecake into her mouth, Elaina propped her elbows on the counter. "Tawny Pia, here's the answer you seek. If Arden was single and went to a thousand therapy sessions, and had an epiphany that he was the cause of our demise, I still wouldn't take him back. I care about him, but everything else inside of me has moved on. The thought of kissing him makes cold shivers run up my spine." She dropped the fork and placed both hands on Tawny's shoulders. "Do not let how I feel about Arden influence how you feel about Grady."

Tawny groaned. "Tell me what to do."

Elaina went back to the cheesecake and savored another creamy bite. "Do you miss having someone in your life? Or do you actually miss Grady?"

"I miss Grady."

"Well then, there's only one thing to do – explore the changes in Grady and see if they're enough. How long will he be in Maine?"

Tawny's mouth dropped open and formed an O. "How did you know he's here?"

Elaina shoved another bite of cheesecake into her mouth.

"Did you do detective work?"

"People who do things on the sly always jump to that conclusion when they're caught red-handed." Elaina bumped Tawny with her arm. "No, I didn't track your every move. The dogs and I came across you and Grady this morning, purely by accident. I wanted a maple latte and there you were, standing in front of the coffee shop, hugging his neck."

"You went all day and didn't say a word."

"Believe me, I had a hard time holding it inside."

Tawny put a hand on her forehead. "You're not going to believe this, but I had a weird sensation come over me when I was with him this morning. I kept turning around, looking for something or someone. I chalked it up to my guilty conscience working overtime."

"Tawny, this is your life. You don't have to feel guilty about the way you handle it."

"I'm so glad you said that."

Ahh, there was more to the story. "Am I going to regret my words?"

* * *

Shortly after diving into the cheesecake and discussing Tawny's feelings for Grady, Tawny had gone into her bedroom – possibly to notify him that she'd outed them.

Elaina decided on a bubble bath. She slid deeply into the warm water, keeping a steady hand on her cup of chamomile tea and sorting through all the shifting-relationships. Steph and Nick had gotten engaged and now owned a home they'd soon move into. The renovations to the Victorian house across the street were almost finished, which meant Grace would relocate too. Should Tawny and Grady work things out the way they wanted, there was a real possibility that Tawn' would pack her suitcases and forward her mail to Ohio.

Stony and Bailey had followed Elaina to the basement and lay on the rug in front of the bathtub, as though they were her security detail.

Elaina whimpered, and Stony rose up to look over the edge of the tub. "It's okay, boy. I'm fine." Palming her face with one hand, she pressed against her eyelids to keep tears from leaking out. She'd known all along that at some point her friends would give their hearts away, and living arrangements would change. She hadn't counted on it being this soon. In a matter of weeks, possibly even days, there might be one permanent resident left in the Four Sassy Chicks Bed and Breakfast. The others would lend an occasional hand with the duties. Elaina could handle most of the responsibility, but she'd miss the daily interaction and closeness. The irony of this situation, and her initial mantra when they first met, pushed into her thoughts – Not my circus, not my monkeys. After getting to know and love the monkeys, she not only wanted their circus, she needed it.

She took a careful sip of tea.

The hum of the water heater warming more water drowned out the footsteps of a visitor.

Tawny appeared in the doorway of the bathroom. "Hey."

Elaina startled. The abrupt movement sloshed tea over the side of the cup and into the bathwater.

Stony popped up to greet his master. Bailey yipped to greet Tawny, but stayed on the soft rug.

Elaina slapped her chest. "Heart, you can start beating again."

"I tried to make noise so I wouldn't scare you. Apparently you were lost in thought." Tawny held a tall, clear glass filled with ice cubes and liquid.

"What are you drinking? Vodka?" Elaina knew it wasn't.

"I'm not a vodka girl. Those Bloody Marys we enjoyed a while back were just okay. I doubt I'll try them again. This, my friend, is good ole H2O." She took a drink and smacked her lips. "I took a break from texting because I was parched."

"Texting? Or sexting?"

"Both and I worked up quite a sweat."

"T.M.I."

"Then why did you ask?" Tawny homed in on Elaina's face. "Have you been crying?"

Elaina looked down at the teacup. "I might be coming down with a cold." It wasn't an outright fib. There could be cold-germs invading her body as she spoke.

"People don't get colds," Tawny snapped her fingers, "just like that."

Elaina slurped her drink.

"What's in the cup? Vodka?" Tawny split a gut laughing.

"Way to toss that back at me. I'll have you know I'm drinking chamomile tea." She rubbed her neck. "My throat feels scratchy." Now she was fibbing. She put the cup down and grabbed a towel. "I should probably tuck in."

"And you should stop pretending you're sick."

"You're not a doctor."

"Yet I know sick people when I see them. You're not sick." Tawny perched on the edge of the tub. "Did my news about Grady upset you?"

"Don't be ridiculous." Elaina coughed.

"Stop that. You're not sick."

"Would I be drinking chamomile tea if I were well?"

"Chamomile helps you to relax. It doesn't relieve cold symptoms." Tawny smiled. "I'm going to be as good for you as Vitamin C right now."

"Oh really?"

"Yes really. I'm not leaving Maine." Tawny tapped Elaina's temple. "I know the hamster in your head is breaking the speed limit on that wheel inside there. One of the many thoughts making him go fast is that you think everyone is abandoning you. The hamster's wrong. I'm not leaving."

"Really, really good to know. I have a question, actually more, but this one is bugging me to death. The big push for us to get into online dating wasn't actually for *us* – it was for me, right?"

Tawny feigned innocence.

* * *

Mouthwatering aromas of coffee and bacon wafted through the air. To Elaina's surprise, it wasn't Steph dressed in the full-length apron.

"Scrambled? Or sunny-side up?"

"Scrambled would be nice." Elaina poured a much-needed cup of coffee. "Thanks, Tawn'." She spared a look at the clock. It was quarter after seven, and Monday to boot. According to the schedule on the refrigerator, Tawny should've been at work fifteen minutes ago. "Did you take a vacation day?"

"I decided to call in sick." Tawny faked a cough. "I caught what you had last night."

"I received a powerful dose of Vitamin C and made a speedy recovery."

Grace shuffled in. "Someone's going to get written up for being late." She plopped down on a chair and took a piece of bacon from the platter.

"No, someone isn't."

Steph wandered in with her red hair piled high in a messy bun. Dressed in a frayed grey t-shirt and jeans with holes in the knees, it was obvious she wasn't headed to the restaurant this morning. She yawned, stretched, and blinked several times in succession when she became aware of Tawny at the stove. "You're making breakfast?"

"I'm not a complete slouch in the kitchen."

"It wasn't an insult. I should've asked what you're doing home."

Elaina answered for Tawny. "She took a sick day."

Steph moved back a step. "You shouldn't be messing with food if you're sick."

Again, Elaina responded. "She's not sick-sick. She's playing sick."

Steph took a coffee mug from the cabinet. "Why the pretense?"

"I had the urge to be bad." Tawny set a serving dish of eggs on the table.

Steph splashed coffee into the mug. "No really. Why?"

They all knew Tawny had a strict work ethic. No way would she play hooky unless it was of the utmost importance.

"I told you. I decided to be bad."

Steph tilted her head. "I'm too tired to wrestle the truth out of you."

"Why are you tired?"

"Why are you ditching your job?"

Tawny set the skillet with bacon grease aside to let it cool. "Call it an adjustment day."

"What kind of adjustment?"

"Sheesh. Tired people shouldn't have the energy to nag." Tawny handed out plates. "Eat while the food's hot." She took a seat at the table. "The adjustment is more of a housing plan."

Grace's brows furrowed. "Are you moving out?"

"No."

"Then color me confused." Grace put her elbows on the table and laced her fingers.

"Elaina and I had an in-depth discussion last night."

"You had a serious discussion without me and Grace?" Steph scooped eggs onto her plate and drizzled maple syrup over them. "Are you two scheming behind our backs?"

Grace stole a forkful of eggs from Steph's plate, and received a swat for her thievery.

"Absolutely not. I'm the only one scheming, and I'm

doing it in front of your backs. Last night, while Elaina was layered with bubbles, I proposed something to keep the four of us together-ish."

"Do tell." Steph made her plate of eggs into a work of art by squirting more syrup until every piece was covered with rich, sticky goodness.

Tawny moved her gaze to Elaina. "I've invited Grady to stay here."

Steph's shock came in the form of choking on a bite of eggs.

"That wouldn't be the least bit awkward." Grace's sarcasm came through loud and clear. "Remember when he had a hissy fit and rutted Elaina's front yard? He pulled onto the lawn and dumped Stony's things all over the place."

"You didn't need to jog my memory. I remember the unpleasant incident."

Steph tossed out something for Tawny to ponder. "Will he turn our little bed and breakfast into a hostile environment?"

A wounded look flitted across Tawny's expression. "I'll assume full liability for his behavior."

Elaina reared up in Tawny's defense. "We support each other, in questionable times and when things go smoothly. Tawny has decided to let Grady back into her life. Whatever the outcome, I'll be there for her. I hope you will be too."

"I can always count on you to have my back."

"It's what friends do."

Steph hit the edge of the table with her thumb at least

a half-dozen times. "I don't mean to be a broken gear in your wheel of happiness. On numerous occasions you said you despised him."

"I said it, and meant it, at the time. My feelings have changed." Tawny sighed. "It's complicated."

Elaina agreed. "Love is never easy or simple. Grace is right to a degree. We know how Grady treated you in the past and having him stay here will be awkward. But handling awkward is the one thing we do well."

* * *

From the moment Grady Westerfield showed up, he radiated peace and joy. It was hard to imagine this charming guy as having been a domineering, perfectionist, pain-in-Tawny's-derriere. However, Elaina believed the things Tawny had said about him over the last several months and chalked up Grady's current demeanor as his get-along front. The true measure of this man would be how he treated Tawny in the coming days. One slip-up and the guy was toast. Elaina gave him a high-cheek smile, but she hoped it served more as a warning than a warming.

Stony showed his delight at seeing Grady again by yowling and rubbing against his legs.

Grady crouched. "I've missed you too." He actually hugged Stony. Pulling to a stand, he worked an arm around Tawny's waist. "I'm tickled to be here."

"Tawny hasn't smiled this much, maybe ever."

Grady kissed the side of Tawny's head. "We've made

significant progress in patching our relationship. I thank God and Tawny, for giving me another chance to get it right."

The suspicion that Grady was saying what Tawn' wanted to hear faded, mostly anyway. "I'm so happy for your guys."

"Thanks, Elaina. Tawny speaks highly of you. I can see why."

"Tawn's a gem. She's made my life better."

"Mine too."

Grace and Steph had been taking it all in.

"Enough with the mushy, blah-blah-blah stuff." Grace jerked her thumb toward the kitchen. "To celebrate this realignment of hearts, Steph and I made hors d'oeurves. Initially, we were going to wait until Philip and Nick could join us, but they won't be around until later. Philip is working in the basement of the mansion across the street." Grace winked at Elaina. "Yes, I call it a mansion. Get over it." She chuckled at Elaina's teasing, pointed look. "Steph's hunk, Nicholas, is working at the restaurant. He'll be home six-ish. Philip and Nick are amazing men. I'm sure you'll all get along great."

Steph informed them she made pinwheels with tortilla wraps, jalapeno ranch cream cheese, prosciutto, onion, and lettuce. "They're delish'. If stuffed mushrooms are your thing, we have a whole tray waiting to be devoured. Grace found a recipe for tiny spinach frittatas. I just tried one." She threw her hands out in dramatic fashion. "They're to die for. Tawny loves my famous glazed chicken drumsticks, so they happened." She started to share the ingredients for the glaze and must've decided their eyes would be more glazed than the chicken if she kept going. "As you can tell, food is my thing."

"Tawny tells me there's a cookbook in the works. How's it coming?"

"Close to being done. We'd like to add one more chapter; something to make our cookbook stand out from all the others."

"Do you have a beverage section?"

"We do."

"Do you have a special-beverage section?"

He'd piqued Steph's interest. "It's special to us."

Grady linked arms with Tawny. "You're the wine club ladies. You could do an entire section with regards to wine – pairing certain wines with the recipes you've created. Add in a bonus – ways to make wine freezes, floats, slushies, ice cubes, and anything else you can think of. According to Tawny, you each like a different kind of wine. Let me see if I remember correctly. Elaina, you like most wines, but prefer blackberry."

"I do." Elaina put her fist out for Grady to knuckle bump.

"Grace, you're all over the white-merlot."

Grace squinted at Tawny. "What else did you tell him?"

Grady answered instead of Tawny. "That when they first met you, you were dressed all in black." He gave her a quick up and down scan. "You're too fair-complected to pull off such a stark color." He motioned to her shirt. "That blue works well with your eyes."

Tawny clutched his bicep. "Who are you?"

They smiled at one another for a few long seconds. He finally pecked her mouth with a soft kiss.

Steph cleared her throat to garner attention. "What did she tell you about me?"

"That you and Nick are madly in love and you're both passionate about food. Oh, and something or other about tricking Elaina into eating..."

Steph filled in the blank. "Succotash."

"She didn't trick me."

"Yes I did. I added all kinds of goodies, also known as kitchen trickery."

The five of them shared a laugh.

A smile of pride spread across Tawny's expression. "I wanted Grady to know you, like I know you. Of course, he'll never truly know you-know you in the way that's special to the four of us."

Steph crossed her arms. "Can you remember what kind of vino I like?"

"Sangria loaded with fruit. Tawny prefers dry red."

Steph looked to his right, to his left, and then up and down. "Do you have a hidden cheat sheet?"

"Nah. Just a good memory."

"Lucky you. Mine could use some tweaking. So you think Nick and I should include the wine sisters?"

"You wanted something to make your book stand out. What better way than with the Four Sassy Chicks?"

Steph wore a dazed expression. No doubt she was already concocting recipes in her head.

Tawny tapped into her wonderment. "What do you think, Steph?"

"I think Grady's a genius."

Grady had the decency to scoff.

"We've been wracking our brains. In two seconds, you broke through the barrier that's been holding us back. Thank you, Grady. Thank you, thank you, thank you."

Grady shook Steph's hand.

His gaze drifted to Elaina and he stared at her for a few blinks, and then lowered his voice to a gentle level. "All of you know Tawny's and my history, yet you're going out of your way to accept me. I know it's more for Tawny's benefit than mine, but I'm grateful for your kindness."

"Getting gooey again. Let's get busy with the yummy." Grace walked side by side with Tawny and Grady. "Did Tawn' tell you Ferdinand is acting up?"

Tawny tried to warn Grace off the subject with a head shake.

Grace didn't take the hint to back off. "Tawn' loves Ole Ferdie. I swear she moans when she's behind the wheel."

Tawny tightened her eyes into a severe squint.

"Why the frown? I'm trying to help. Maybe Grady can check Ferdinand to find out what's wrong with him."

"Do you think he wants to work on a vehicle that makes me moan?"

Grady pealed with laughter.

Everyone, Tawny in particular, seemed stumped. According to the things she'd said about her ex, he'd grown too serious over the past ten years and rarely laughed.

"I'd be happy to take a look at Ferdinand."

Tawny snagged a spinach frittata from the plate and held it out for Grady to take a bite.

He made eyes at Tawny. "Mmm." It could've been for the frittata, but probably not.

Instead of getting their own plates of food, Tawny and Grady continued to forage from the serving dishes.

Tawny stuck a toothpick in a mushroom and let Grady have the first taste.

Again, he said, "Mmm." His eyes rolled back in his head.

When Tawny and Grady shared a chicken drumstick, and made pleasured sounds, Elaina looked at Grace.

Grace mouthed the word they'd expressed earlier about Grady staying there, "Awkward."

Steph finally said, "Get a room."

"Good idea." Tawny winked and took Grady by the arm.

As soon as they were out of the kitchen, Grace double-checked to make sure they were out of earshot. "Did they have food-sex in front of us?"

Elaina laughed so hard she snorted. Steph did the same. When they were done yukking it up, Grace said, "They didn't even use protection." The silly comment sent all three into hysterics again.

Grace put together a plate of appetizers for Philip and made a beeline across the street.

Steph toyed with a pinwheel. "The next time I make these I'll cut back on the jalapeno and add more onion. Maybe a little more Ranch dressing would jazz them up too."

Tawny reappeared in the kitchen.

"I noticed you went upstairs instead of to your room."

"Grady's a paying customer – hence, his own room."

"You're making him pay?"

Tawny pulled at her bottom lip with her teeth. "In more ways than one."

"I underestimated you, woman." Steph hit the button for the garbage disposal to chomp the scraps of food she'd scraped from the plates. "You're putting him to the test, aren't you?"

"It's necessary. And it isn't for him alone. It's also for me. I have to know if this sudden thaw was spawned from desperation and a lack of sex."

"To make sure a midnight rendezvous won't be easy to pull off you put him on the third floor." Elaina was well-aware that being intimate could derail clear thinking. She was happy Tawny chose to distance herself from that temptation.

"Texting back and forth was one thing; having him in my personal space again, is something altogether different. I've had moments of pure panic."

There was no panic when you were feeding each other. Elaina would keep that tidbit out of the conversation. She put the remaining mushrooms in a plastic container. "I can relate. When I'm near Arden, my pulse tries to beat itself out of my chest and I break out in a cold sweat."

"Yet you haven't told him to stay out of your life."

"I've told him. He just doesn't listen. It's like you said earlier, Tawn', it's complicated. Unlike you, I can say with complete certainty, the things Arden stirs up aren't from a desire to get back together."

"See, that's a big grey area for me too. Before I can let Grady back into my heart…and in my bed…I have to identify the underlying cause of why I'm allowing this to happen in the first place. Is this sudden yearning for him born from fear of starting over with someone else? I have to know."

Grace returned. "What did I miss?"

"Tawny wants to make Grady work for it."

Steph received a poke in the ribs from Tawny.

Chapter Ten

~ Always another surprise! ~

"Good morning, Sassy Chicks." Grady bent and planted a kiss on Tawny's lips. "You look beautiful."

Tawny fluffed the back of her hair. "I know, right?"

"You made coffee and bacon."

"Steph fried the bacon. Elaina made the coffee."

Grady took a strip of bacon.

Elaina handed him a cup of coffee. "Do you take it with milk and sugar?"

"I take it in a travel mug."

Elaina threw Tawny a questioning look.

"Are you leaving?" There was a sudden crack of nervousness in Tawny's voice.

"I'm not leaving-leaving. I wanted to ask if you and Elaina would accompany me on a walk."

"Me and Elaina?"

Steph piped up. "There are two more Sassy Chicks, you know."

"I'm sorry for not extending the invitation to you and

Grace. It's just that the sidewalk is only so wide. And I have something important I want to run by Tawny and Elaina."

"We could walk behind you. Grace and I involve ourselves in important stuff too."

"It's not a slight."

"Quit giving him the business, Steph."

Steph smirked. "Are you going to ask Elaina to be a witness to...?"

There was an unspoken, yet loud threat woven through Tawny's glare.

Steph put her teeth together in an impish grin. "I couldn't resist." She stretched to look out the window. "It's not warm enough for me to go prancing around the neighborhood anyway, so go ahead and walk your legs off."

"I second that." Grace cracked a boiled egg and began peeling the shell. "In two days it's Easter. You wouldn't know it by the temperature."

A cold front had moved in to replace the warm spell. It had been great while it lasted.

Brimming with curiosity, Elaina hopped up from the chair. "I'll get our coats."

Following Tawny and Grady out the back door, Elaina mischievously raised and lowered her eyebrows at Grace and Steph.

Outside it was cold enough to see your breath.

Grady held onto Tawny and his coffee mug. Elaina felt like a third wheel.

A half-block from home, Grady stopped and began

the discussion. "Tawny, you love it in Maine." He swept his gaze around the area. "Elaina, you've counted on Tawny being here. I can't in good conscience take her back to Ohio. That would be wrong."

Tawny had forewarned Elaina what the conversation was about. Elaina tried to appear as though she had no clue where he was going with this.

"I find myself in unfamiliar territory." Grady cleared his throat. "Should things keep getting better between Tawny and me, our separate addresses could become an issue. And I don't want to do anything to jeopardize our improvement."

Tawny inched the zipper on her coat higher to block out the biting wind that was sweeping in off the Atlantic. "Can we walk and talk? My feet are getting cold standing here."

Grady kissed the side of Tawny's head. "A walk might not have been the best choice."

"Fresh air is always a good choice."

Tawny inclined her head toward Elaina. "Just so you know, she spouts a lot of health stuff."

"I have an occasional moment, but you have a ton of them." Elaina used her hands to mimic a scale going up and down. "I tilt toward donuts some days, and others, I'm all about celery." She gave them a goofy smile. "Grady, you were saying?"

"This is a highly unusual request and the reason I wanted it to remain between the three of us, is in case you give me the thumbs-down. The more people involved the higher degree of embarrassment I'd suffer."

Grady stopped walking again and turned to Tawny. "You've told me you feel as though you aren't pulling your weight around here."

"I do carry around a certain amount of guilt for not doing my fair share."

"I'm doing fine." Elaina corrected, "We're doing fine."

"You're too nice to say otherwise."

Grady squeezed Tawny's hand. "I'd like to put something out there for both of you to consider. If you say yes, I'll be one of the happiest men on the planet. If the answer is no, I'll have to deal with it."

Tawny played it to the hilt. "There are laws against polygamy."

Grady's eyebrows scrunched together. Then it hit him that she'd made a joke. He laughed until he had to blow his nose. "I don't remember you being this funny, Tawny. I love it."

"I've always had a sense of humor. You were just too busy to…" Tawny pressed her lips together.

Elaina gave Tawny big points for suppressing the curt reply.

"I didn't appreciate what an extraordinary woman you are until I no longer had you." He pulled her close and gave her a kiss so steamy it should've taken the chill out of the air.

With kisses like that, Tawny and Grady wouldn't be staying in separate rooms for long. Elaina looked around to keep from staring, feeling even more like a third wheel.

When they parted, Grady apologized. "Sorry for the PDA."

"As long as Tawny's good with it, so am I. But let's get down to brass tacks."

Grady swallowed hard, making his Adam's apple bob. "Tawny and I are going to make it. I know we are, and I want to make her happy for the rest of our lives. Our home is officially in Ohio, but I could sell the house and move here."

"You'd do that?" Tawny still pretended she was hearing this for the first time.

"I would do anything for you."

"What about your job? You have years invested with the company."

"They'll buy me out, and I'd sock the money into my 40lk…for us."

"Let's say you relocate to Portland. Would you buy a house or rent?"

Grady hesitated and transferred his gaze to Elaina. "I get that four people are making a living from your bed and breakfast, and you can't afford to dole out money to one more. I have a proposition." His attention reverted back to Tawny. "For room and board only, I could do your share of the work and be the handyman."

Tawny pulled her hat down so low you could barely see her eyes. "You're willing to sell the home we raised our boys in and quit a good paying job to become a handyman?" Not allowing him space to answer, she added, "Who are you? And what have you done with Grady?"

Grady smiled at her over the edge of the travel mug. "I love you. I miss you. I want you in my life. Tawny, I'm willing to do whatever I can to be with you."

This was a poignant and private moment that should've been between just Tawny and Grady. Elaina wanted to sneak off, but any sudden movement would shatter the warmth and bring them back to the reality of a chilly day in Maine.

Tawny grasped Elaina's arm with a tight grip. "What do you think?"

"There's only one thing you can do – follow your heart. Tawn', what Grady's offering sounds like a win-win, even if it occasionally includes axle grease."

Tawny's face became a huge question mark until realization dawned.

The memory of them capitalizing on Grady's weakness – an aversion to certain textures, one of which included axle grease – made Elaina stifle a laugh by clamping her lips shut. Shortly after Tawny and the others had moved in to her home in Ohio, Grady had misbehaved, and they paid him back with grease on his door handles, trash can, and welcome mat.

Grady's gaze popped back and forth between Elaina and Tawny, as though trying to figure out what was transpiring between them.

Tawny pushed into Elaina. "I don't know what I'd do without you." She smiled at Grady. "I don't know what I'd do without you either. Sooo..." She spared a quick glance at Elaina, before giving Grady what he wanted. "You'd be a valuable asset at The Four Sassy Chicks Bed and Breakfast."

Grady's smile went from ear to ear, but then his mouth became a thin line. "There's one small catch."

Tawny gave him a half-second death stare.

"Don't worry. It's all good. Along with being your maintenance man, I'd also like a side business of my own, using my web design and graphics skills. That way, I'd have some disposable income."

Since Grady and Tawny wanted Elaina's third-wheel presence, she cut in. "For trips to see your boys?"

Grady's smile returned. "Yes."

"You lovebirds should go see Bo and Quentin in the near future."

Tawny lifted one eyebrow. "You've encouraged Grace to fly off into the wild blue yonder. Now you're doing the same to me and Grady. What are you up to?"

"I want you to be happy, that's all."

"We want the same for you."

Elaina pivoted on her heels and looked toward the bed and breakfast. She felt around the front of her coat until the outline of the anchor necklace met her fingers. "I couldn't be happier."

"Your pants should be on fire right about now for lying."

Grady wrinkled his forehead at Tawny. "She said she's happy, Tawny."

"That's not what I heard."

"I distinctly heard the word happy."

"And I distinctly heard her soul crying out for Jess."

Elaina rolled her eyes.

* * *

"You're going to be our handyman?"

"I won't look hot in a tool belt, but I know how to fix things."

Steph flushed with embarrassment. "I didn't mean to suggest you didn't meet the physical requirements. It's just that Tawny never mentioned you were handy."

Nick barged through the back door, toting three stuffed-to-the-max plastic bags with the restaurant logo on the front. "I come bearing gifts."

Steph helped with the bags. "Men. I just love 'em."

Nick gave her a weird look.

"Well I do. You brought food so I don't have to make dinner. Grady has volunteered to be Mr. Fix-it for the Four Sassy Chicks. And Philip has used his photography talent to give our little enterprise another personal touch." Taking Nick by the hand, Steph led him to the foyer. "Have a look-see at his recent work of art."

Everyone gathered around.

"What's this?" Elaina hawkeyed the photo she didn't remember posing for.

Grace worked her finger around Philip's belt loop. "This big lug painted all of us in front of the mansion. Pretty cool, eh?"

Grady squinted. "I'm in there too. When did you do this?"

Philip clicked his tongue. "It's something I put together today."

In the painting, Elaina had been placed on the far left side. Philip had left an odd grey area next to her. She moved her head one way, and then the other, coming to an uncomfortable conclusion about the painting. "You forgot to blob some paint here."

Philip slung an arm around Elaina. "It's a deliberate void. Wait. Void isn't the right word. It's a deliberate empty space." He stretched his mouth wide with a wince.

Grace shook her head. "Epic fail, Philip. Elaina, what he's trying to say, is when Jess returns…"

"Oh for the love of Pete, you've all gone insane." The grumpiness spilled out of Elaina and she couldn't stop it. "Jess is in a relationship with his music, not me. When it comes to him and me, there are two words to describe our story – The End."

Grace wrinkled her nose. "Does anyone else detect a massive amount of cynicism spewing out of our happy girl?"

Tawny got in on the act. "Stop spewing. You're grossing me out."

Elaina ignored the good-natured ribbing. "It was considerate of you to leave space for him, Philip." Less and less thrilled with the Jess-agenda everyone seemed to push these days, she was one breath away from telling them to stop it. Lately, she questioned the depth of her feelings for Jess and got the same answer every time – there had been no love, only a desire to be loved. Silently she groaned at her proclivity to mix up the two. How was a woman supposed to identify her true emotions after having been in a long-term, unpleasant relationship?

Tawny snapped her fingers in front of Elaina. "Come back to earth."

Elaina forced herself to focus. "I never left."

"You were thinking too hard about something. Wanna fill us in?"

"I was thinking this painting will be great advertisement for the art gallery. Guests will inquire about the magnificent home in the background and we'll send them across the street."

Tawny sniffed the air. "Does anyone else smell burning pants?"

The only one who paid attention to the liar-liar-pants-on-fire insinuation was Elaina. She bunched her face into a smirk.

Grace clapped. "It's finally time to unveil the mansion."

Philip informed them that the downstairs was finished. He was most proud of the front room that displayed his handiwork. "One bedroom is done on the second floor. The rest of the rooms will be finished as time and finances allow."

"The place rocks; except for the creepy basement." Grace made a face. "I refuse to go down there."

"Come on, Grace. Show us the whole house. We'll be with you." Elaina almost said they'd carry her bodily to the basement if she refused to accompany them.

Grace moved her head back and forth like a petulant child refusing to eat broccoli. "N-O."

"You have to conquer your fear. If you don't, every noise or squeak will freak you out." Elaina braced her hand on the small of Grace's back and pushed her forward. "Start walking, sista."

"You're a pain."

"And a happy girl, right?"

* * *

"If anything jumps out at me and I end up in Coronary Care at the hospital, it's your fault." Grace clutched the handrail so hard, it was a wonder she didn't yank it out of the wall.

"I'm pretty sure you won't visit Coronary Care, but you might find yourself in the ER with another twisted ankle, thanks to these rickety steps." Elaina glanced over her shoulder at Tawny, who was grinning like a Cheshire cat.

"One twisted ankle was enough." Grace smacked Philip on the back. "New basement steps before I move in."

He retorted, "Yes, boss."

Nick and Grady were at the back of the line and probably elbowing each other at Philip's remark.

In the dimly-lit, musty basement they met in the open area near the antiquated furnace.

Philip wrapped his arms around Grace from behind. "How did you twist your ankle?"

"Long story short, I had a clumsy moment."

"Lengthen it just a little. I want to know."

Grace looked all around, still uneasy with her surroundings. "Cody called from Italy. In a rush to get downstairs to answer the phone, I missed the last couple steps. I'm fortunate to only have suffered an ankle injury." She touched her nose. "I came close to face-planting."

Steph shined a small flashlight in Grace's face

spotlighting a scowl. She clicked it off. "I missed the trip to the hospital and the pharmacy afterward. Apparently they had more fun than they should have, given the state of Grace's ankle."

"A sprained ankle isn't what I'd call fun, Steph."

"I meant how you turned a painful fiasco into an adventure."

Grace scratched her head. "My memory must be fuzzy. I don't recall it being anything but a nuisance."

Elaina explained that Grace had been on powerful meds on the way home from the hospital and had conked out in the backseat, while she and Tawny went into the drugstore to get her prescription filled.

Grady asked what kind of shenanigans they could possibly have been up to in a drugstore.

"They told me it involved...," Steph stopped mid-sentence.

"Involved what?"

It was too dark to see whether Steph blushed when she said, "Personal lubricant."

Grady wasn't amused. "What did they do with personal lubricant?"

"They didn't use it to skate down the aisles, if that's what you're thinking."

Nick laughed like Steph had said the funniest thing he'd ever heard.

Elaina had a feeling Grady and Tawny's progress just hit a snag, so she did what any good friend would do – fibbed. "I had the hots for this guy. Tawny and I bumped into him near a display involving lubricant. It goes without saying that he wasn't buying it for me and him. As soon as Tawny and I were out of his sight and far enough away he couldn't hear us, we lost it. I remember getting a side ache from laughing so hard."

Tawny cleared her throat.

Elaina sighed, knowing what was about to happen.

"The thing about besties, they try to smooth over bumpy moments for their friends. Thanks, Elaina, I appreciate the less-controversial version. Grady, this isn't a confessional, but I'm going to own up to the truth." Tawny cleared her throat a second time. "I'm the one who had the hots for one of the doctors at the hospital. He was an Australian with a sexy accent. We spotted him at the pharmacy with a tube of lube. A minute later, a nurse from the hospital linked arms with him. My fantasy crashed and burned, right then and there. Elaina lobbed a smart remark at him about the lube and we high-tailed it out of there."

"Oh."

"That's all you have to say?"

"No. There's more floating around in my head, but I'm smart enough to keep it there."

"While I'm telling all, I also want you to know I dated a car salesman and a dog warden."

There wasn't a trace of cockiness in Grady's tone. "Anyone else?"

"Uh, let's see." Tawny tapped her chin. "Nope. That's it."

"Since you came clean, it's my turn. I dated a waitress twice. Nice gal. I hated every minute of being with her though."

"Why?"

"She wasn't you."

It was a tender moment, meant for just Tawny and Grady, but Elaina was happy to have witnessed it. At least this time, she wasn't a third wheel; more like a seventh wheel.

Everyone smothered Tawny and Grady with hugs.

Elaina whispered to Tawny, "I believe the man is truly in love with you."

Tawny squeezed Elaina tight. "He surprises me at every turn."

"Now that we have that out of the way, shall we finish this eerie expedition?" Grace yanked Elaina's coat sleeve. "This place really does give me the creeps."

"Steph, why weren't you with your friends when Grace hurt her ankle?"

Elaina was amazed that Nick had latched onto what should've been an insignificant detail in the conversation.

Tawny bumped Steph's shoe with her boot. "It's best to tell him."

"I was at the Four Sassy Chicks Bed and Breakfast." Steph's voice trailed off and it was difficult to hear when she added, "Before it had that name."

"You were here?"

Steph stretched her neck from side to side and cracked her knuckles, stalling. "I followed a meat cutter from Ohio to Maine, okay?"

Philip tried to hold in a laugh, but it erupted from him loud and hearty.

Grace pushed at his chest.

"What? How is Steph following a meat cutter not funny?"

"When you put it like that..."

Nick saw the humor it in as well. He bounced with a chuckle and then planted his hands firmly on Steph's waist. "If you hadn't followed the guy, we never would've met. You don't have to delve into the details, sweetheart. Just know that his loss is my gain."

Philip got in on the act. "What skeletons do you have in your closet, Grace?"

"Don't say skeletons. That's just plain mean. You know I'm on the fringe of hysteria down here."

Elaina was worried that Grace would think of her late husband. She was sure Philip hadn't meant to gear her in that direction with his innocent question.

"Let me reword it. Do you have any men stashed in the closet?" "

"Now you're being ridiculous."

"I can go back to saying skeletons, if ya want."

Grace muttered something under her breath. "Dalton isn't a *skeleton*. He was a red-blooded, good-looking specimen who ignored me in school, but paid attention to me after his divorce. I thought we had something. We didn't."

"Dalton, huh?"

"Deal with it. Or not."

"Wow. Ouch."

Grace straightened from a slouch. "I loved Brince, dated Dalton, and pretended to be attracted to Officer Ted. Now I'm here with you. If my past bothers you, this is your one and only chance to bellyache."

"I won't ask about Ted." Philip sifted air through his teeth. "What are your feelings for me?"

"You already know them."

"Tell me again."

Grace rubbed the muscles at the base of her neck. "After I lost Brince, I thought my life was over too. I got a second whammy when Cody moved out. I cried all the time and could barely function. These amazing women saw me crying my heart out in the jewelry store. They could've easily ignored me. Instead, they took me under their wings and shored me up when I was at my lowest. Little by little, I started to breathe again. Thanks to them I got the strength to go out with Dalton and make eyes at Ted. Then we moved to Maine. And there you were – a long-haired creative rebel, who won my heart right away."

"I'm different from the other men you've been attracted to."

"Yes you are."

Elaina noted the urgency in Grace's voice for them to move on. Grace would always love Brince, but she'd made room in her heart for Philip. That was nothing short of a miracle. "Unlike you three, I don't have to confess anything. I'm free as a bird."

"We have two tattoos that say otherwise. What one does, we all do." Tawny directed a finger to Elaina. "Speaketh now or be locked in this dudgeon forever."

"Oh no! Not the creepy basement," Elaina joked.

"We had to squirm under the microscope and so do you."

"Seriously, it's a boring narrative."

Philip told Elaina he seriously wanted to hear it.

"Prepare yourself for a yawn-fest." Elaina mentioned Arden, but she didn't highlight his penchant to dominate everything and everyone. She touched on Michael Rexx, the guy she'd met at the gym in Ohio, whom she dated until he reconnected with his ex-wife. From there, she moved on to be attracted to Officer Chad Ferguson, who came to the bed and breakfast after she set off the security alarm. "Chad was offered his dream job in the Big Apple and severed ties with me. Jess came on scene when he needed a quiet space to finish his album."

"We sure go through men," Tawny stated.

Grady inhaled sharply.

"Just so you know, Grady dear, I say inappropriate stuff all the time."

Elaina agreed with a nod. "She absolutely does. It's part of her charm."

Grace coughed to gather their attention. While Elaina had been going through the doldrums of her mostly non-existent dating life, Grace had put on the infamous catwoman mask.

Chapter Eleven

~ *Spying on the ham!* ~

"I'm sorry, sir, I don't understand what you're saying." Elaina wiggled a finger in her ear.

The caller handed the phone to someone else. A clear, crisp voice took over. "Ma'am, my friends Sergei and Alexei are touring the United States and Canada. They'll be visiting Portland on Monday and will need a place to stay for one night. Tuesday morning they'll board the ferry to Yarmouth, Nova Scotia. Do you have rooms available?"

Elaina scanned the reservation ledger. "I do."

"Awesome."

"Will you be joining them as well?"

"No, Ma'am. They're on their own."

"Then we might have a small problem."

"The language barrier?"

"Yes, sir."

"It shouldn't be an issue. Sergei knows some conversational English. Should he not grasp something, he has a translating device."

"And Alexei?"

"Alexei tries to speak English, but frankly, he botches more than he gets right. He once called me a goat instead of George. Maybe it was intentional." The man known as George laughed at his own joke and then spoke in fluent Russian to his friends.

Elaina crossed her fingers; hoping things would go as smoothly as George seemed to think. "Will they require transportation from the airport?"

"They will. That's one reason they chose your place; the other being the name of your establishment. Who wouldn't want to stay at a place called Four Sassy Chicks? It's quite the hook."

She laughed lightly and asked for flight details.

After the call ended, a dozen thoughts raced through Elaina's head, but they were interrupted by Grace.

"I need a new phone. This blasted thing has to be charged every day." Grace plugged it into the special USB outlet that could hold up to three phones. "Why the weird look on your face?"

"I just took a reservation for Alexei and Sergei."

"Oooo. Foreigners. Their names suggest twins. And possibly weightlifters?"

Elaina shrugged. "All I know is they're Russian and speak very little English."

"Maybe we should learn a few Russian words in advance."

"The task is yours."

Steph wandered in and snatched the grocery list out from under a refrigerator magnet. "What are you assigning Grace to do?"

"Learn Russian by Monday."

Steph's reddish-brown eyebrows crinkled into a strict V. "Because?"

"She needs a challenge."

"No really. Why?"

"She wants to become a spy."

Steph did a half-eye roll. "Whatever. You two have fun making up stories. I'm headed to the grocery to get things for our Easter dinner."

Grace blocked Steph's exit. "What are we having?"

Steph said something that made Elaina and Grace exchange confused looks.

"Come again?"

"I said ham in Russian."

Elaina made big eyes at Steph. "You know Russian?"

"I know how to say ham."

"Of all the words in the Russian language, you happen to know ham – the food you're preparing for Easter."

Steph slung her purse on her shoulder. "Don't ask me how I know, I just do."

"Maybe you lived in Russia in a former life."

"And maybe you were a nag in another life. No. Wait. You're a nag now." Steph sidestepped Grace. "The boss lady told you to learn Russian. Time's a-wastin'." She exited through the back door and you could still hear her laughing as she walked through the breezeway and into the garage.

"We certainly live up to our name." Elaina filled the coffee pot reservoir with water. "Apparently Alexei and

Sergei wanted to stay here because we're The Four Sassy Chicks."

"What do you suppose they expect from us?"

Elaina attempted the Russian word for ham.

Grace busted out laughing. "I can see ham will be our go-to word for the next few days."

Nick sauntered down the stairs. "Good, you're making coffee. I could use a jolt of caffeine. I just got off the phone with Norma. She's taking a sick day."

"Does she have the flu?" Elaina hit the start button on the coffeemaker.

"Nope."

"A bad cold?"

"Nope." Nick sounded more irked with every reply. "She asked if she could take family medical leave."

Elaina tried to figure out why Norma would need family medical leave. She had two ex-spouses that she wouldn't give the time of day, let alone take off work for. Like Elaina, she didn't have kids. Her parents were getting up there in years, but they seemed to be in good health – although with aging parents anything was possible.

Nick ran a hand over his chin. "I can't believe she had the audacity to ask for time off because Lula has been moping around."

"Aww."

Nick's forehead creased into an accordion of lines. "Elaina, don't say aww. It's a cat, for crying out loud."

"Lula is Norma's cat-child. Unless you have a cat, you wouldn't understand." The coffee pot gurgled to completion. Elaina took three mugs from the cabinet.

"I can't pay her medical leave for a cat."

"Is she still your best worker?"

"Yes, but this falls under the realm of insane."

Elaina passed the coffee pot to Nick. "Pay her for the time off. It doesn't have to be for medical reasons. In the long run, you'll be doing yourself a favor. Norma loves to waitress. She also loves Lula. Don't make her choose between the two."

Nick eyed Elaina for an inordinate amount of time and grumbled under his breath that if he didn't love being a restaurant owner so much, he'd sell the place and live a normal life. "I hate that you're right."

Grace peered over the edge of her cup. "Sometimes you have to bend the rules for the greater good."

"I'll have to swear Norma to secrecy. If word gets out that I paid her to stay home with her cat, the other employees will call off to be with their dogs or birds."

Elaina said the Russian word for ham.

Grace sputtered coffee into the air.

* * *

Elaina escorted the group of seven into the pew. Kneeling, she closed her eyes and bowed her head. Easter was a time to rejoice and seek guidance. Boy did she need guidance. First, she prayed for her parents and then began a long, quiet conversation with the man upstairs. *I'm a huge clutter of confusion, Lord. On the outside, I'm the same as always. Inside, well, you're familiar with my struggles. Everything is changing. My friends have found their soul mates. I'm beyond happy for them. They deserve as much joy and grace as you can provide. But this third-wheel, and sometimes seventh-wheel thing, gets old and makes me sad. I know you have a plan all laid out for me. If I'm to meet someone, could you make it sooner than later? We're not supposed to know what the future holds, but a small sign would work wonders for my soul.* The rest of what she wanted to say had to be put on hold, since the first notes of the entrance hymn brought the parishioners to their feet.

The lyrics from *Amazing Grace* bellowed from the choir loft.

Steph drifted forward to catch Elaina's eyes. A smile passed between them as they remembered Steph singing the wrong words to the song all those months ago. So much had taken place since then and Elaina was grateful for each moment, regardless of how crazy and trying some of those things had been and still were.

After mass, a smile touched Elaina's lips at a sudden and unexpected feeling of peace.

Tawny assessed Elaina. "What happened in there?"

"I don't understand the question."

"The entire time I saw your lips moving, like you were talking to yourself." Tawny rolled up a church bulletin and whacked Elaina on the arm. "Something's troubling you."

"I'm not troubled."

"Good thing you're no longer in church. All that fibbing would bring the rafters down on your head."

Everyone else had walked ahead. Grady turned to locate Tawny. He retraced his steps. His actions prompted Elaina to blurt the truth. "I asked for divine intervention when it comes to men."

"Maybe your guardian angel will guide your fingers to click into that online dating site."

"My guardian angel just scoffed. Wait. That was me."

"For someone who's only forty-four, you're sure set in your ways."

"Said the woman who wanted to see and feel the chemistry in-person."

"I do recall saying something along that line." Tawny ditched the humor. "There's someone extraordinary in store for you, Elaina. You'll meet him when you least expect it and in a way you didn't count on."

Please don't let it be Sergei or Alexei. Maine was where her heart was, not Moscow.

* * *

Steph's eyes watered. "I used too much hot sauce and not enough pineapple. I wanted sweet ham, with just enough fire to make it interesting." She stuck out her tongue. "Do I have blisters?"

"I don't see any." Nick stabbed a slab of the ham from the platter, cut a small piece, and popped it into his mouth. He chewed with a smile. "It's delicious, sweetheart." A few seconds later, the after-burn caught up and he grabbed his water glass.

"Note to self: a little hot sauce goes a long way."

Tawny didn't resist the opportunity to poke fun. "Note to self: when Steph isn't looking, hide the generous slice of ham on my plate under the garlic green beans and instead pleasure my mouth with rabbit."

Steph's temper rose to the surface. "I didn't make rabbit!"

Tawny reached behind her to the long narrow table that normally held an array of house plants, but now held eight Easter baskets. "I meant the dark chocolate kind."

Steph wadded her cloth napkin and threw it at Tawny.

The commotion in the dining room stirred Stony's interest. He placed his muzzle on the half-door meant to keep pets out of the food and eating areas.

"It's all good, Stone-man. Steph didn't put out an eye when she assaulted me with her napkin." Tawny cupped her mouth and whispered loudly. "She's mad at herself for messing up the ham."

Steph held up a butter knife with a snarky threat. "This can hurt as much as a steak knife, maybe more. Just saying."

Tawny continued to project a whisper. "Stony, when I give the word, sink your teeth into her ankle not the ham."

Steph's eyes flared open. "We're all guilty of sneaking table scraps to the dogs. DO NOT...I repeat...DO NOT give Stony or Bailey any of this ridiculous meat. I don't even want to think about what it would do to their bellies."

"Or to the carpet." Grace earned herself a twitchy scowl from Steph.

Grady covered his ham with mushroom gravy. Braving a bite, he chewed and waited. "Try the gravy technique. It dulls the heat."

"Couldn't hurt." Right away Nick apologized to Steph. "No offense, hon'."

She tapped her fingers on the table. "None taken."

"Aren't you two just the cutest?" Tawny removed the decorative foil wrapper and bit the head off the chocolate rabbit.

Grady shook his head at Tawny antics and asked Steph how the cookbook was coming.

"It's almost finished, thanks to you. The idea of specialty drinks in conjunction with the Four Sassy Chicks was brilliant."

Nick said that they went to work on Grady's suggestion right away. "I think you'll be pleased."

Steph dipped the end of a dinner roll in gravy. "Nick and I brainstormed some unusual concoctions. We haven't had an opportunity to try them. Since today is a rare occasion where we're all together, do you mind if we use you for taste-testers?"

"I'm in." Elaina pushed away her nearly full plate.

Tawny forearmed Elaina. "Liquid courage to help you with what's NOT troubling you?"

Grace sat up a little straighter. "I knew ou were in a snit."

"I'm NOT in a snit."

Grace ignored Elaina's rapid defense. "Is it Jess? Is his lack of communication still getting under your skin? Do you want me and Philip to travel to Virginia and knock some sense into him? We'd be happy to do it. Wouldn't we, Philip?"

Philip grabbed the gravy boat and poured gravy on his ham. "Four questions without taking a breath. That has to be a new record." He handed the gravy boat to Grace with a smirk and then smiled at Elaina. "Jess is bigger than me. If Grace and I combine our muscles we could put him in a chokehold."

"It's generous of you to risk life and limb, but it would be wasted effort. I decided this morning in church that Jess is history."

"That explains a lot. What if he showed up at the door this very second and begged you to forgive him for being an ass?" Tawny's expression etched with mischief, yet there were undertones of empathy in her voice.

"I'd forgive him."

"Would you and Jess pick up where you left off?"

"No way. Hey, Steph, I'm ready to try one of those drinks." Elaina put a hand on her throat. "I'm parched."

"You're also trying to circumvent a lengthier discussion."

"I'm also trying to hold onto a fragile thread of dignity. I've drawn a line in the sand and I won't allow Jess to cross."

"Atta girl. That's the strong woman Steph has bent my ear about all this time. I've seen you weaken over the past few months, Elaina, and I knew exactly what was happening. No matter how tough we think we are, sooner or later the damage of divorce takes a toll. The destruction has to be identified and repaired.

Until we do both, we put on a brave face and pretend we're fine. Regarding Jess..." Nick reached across the table and patted Elaina's arm. "When we don't want to acknowledge someone else's decision, we fight closing the door on that relationship. Deep down, Jess probably knew he didn't have the capacity to fill your need. Jess's actions spoke more loudly than the words he was too afraid to say. In my opinion, he was a bad decision. Let me clarify – I don't think he's a bad guy."

Elaina was blown away by Nick's profound thoughts. "Thank you, Nick. I appreciate your honest take on things. You're right – Jess isn't a bad guy, he just wasn't the one for me. I jumped into the romance wading pool heart-first. That isn't my normal modus operandi."

Grace asked, "Who says things like modus operandi?"

Tawny answered, "Cops."

"On TV they say M.O. I'm pretty sure they do the same in real life."

With her thumb, Elaina pointed to herself. "This dork seldom abbreviates."

"You're a lovable dork."

"*Lovable dork* should be your next tattoo." At Elaina's shuttered lashes, Tawny grinned.

Nick brought them back to the matter at hand. "Perhaps Jess's appeal was how different he was from Arden." He wiped the corners of his mouth with his napkin. "Or maybe you needed for someone other than your best friends to pay attention to you for a while."

Elaina's tightly held emotions splintered. Hot tears rushed to scald her eyes. Within seconds, she was wrapped in twelve caring arms. She pushed at them to make them leg go. "I'm okay. The ham was too spicy and made me cry."

Laughter superseded the tears.

"You really ARE going to be okay, Samuels," Nick gently quipped. "You have us and your sense of humor to get you through."

"When you need a good cry, eat leftover ham." Steph playfully wrinkled her nose. "Let the beverage service begin."

Elaina excused herself from the group to change out of her church clothes. Closing the basement door behind her, she flicked off the light and sagged against the wall, taking comfort in the darkness. "You're not weak, you're strong." She repeated the pep talk several times, letting it sink in. "I am strong and there's nothing wrong with giving in to moments of weakness." She finished her trek down the stairs and into the bathroom. Studying her reflection in the mirror, Elaina lifted her chin. "You have a good head on your shoulders. It's time to start using it."

Dressed in jeans and a t-shirt, she joined the drink experiment.

"Try this. It's not your typical glass of wine. This one has tiny bits of pulp." Steph described it as a sweet red vintage, with vodka and lemon-lime soda."

Elaina took a sip and licked her lips. "Yum. You failed to mention another ingredient."

"You noticed."

"How could I not? Whatever the secret ingredient is, it gives the drink something extra special."

Steph lowered her voice to keep the additive top secret.

"There are three something-specials in there. We blended tangerines and fresh cranberries with orange juice."

Elaina finished the sample and held out the glass. "Fill 'er up."

A broad smile washed across Steph's face. "Nick thought the pulp would turn people off."

"Tell Nick it turns me on instead. You have to name the drink something spicy."

"I'm not calling it ham."

"I meant spicy-sensual."

Steph flounced away with a giggle.

The vacancy beside Elaina was filled by Tawny.

"Take a look." Tawny swiveled a martini glass in her hand. "Nick dipped the rim in melted chocolate and then poured in vodka and two chocolate liqueurs. He turned his back so I couldn't see what else he included. Those two are wily mixologists." She scraped some of the chocolate off the glass with her teeth. "A girl could get toasted easily with a few of these."

"I should get toasted." Elaina squeezed her face into a goofy grin. "I have Russians coming tomorrow."

Tawny raised and lowered her eyebrows. "Are you thinking what I'm thinking?"

"Seldom."

Their laughs blended together.

"What are you thinking, Tawn'?"

"Two spies sneaking their way across the US, gathering Intel from unsuspecting people."

"That didn't cross my mind for a second. My concern is big men with big personalities."

"Who just happen to be spies?"

"Okay, we'll go with that." Elaina nudged Tawny with an elbow. "What do Russian men like to eat?"

"Bear."

Elaina tilted her head and gave her wisecracking friend the really-look.

"Let's find out." Tawny used her phone and typed Elaina's question word for word into Google. "They're crazy about sausage, tea, and something called tvorog."

"Which is?"

"Hold on. I'll check."

Steph carried a tray with several drinks and stopped in front of Elaina and Tawny. "I have your pulpy wine. Before you get jiggy with it, Nick wants your opinion on another drink." She pointed to the shot-size plastic cups on the tray.

"Dare we inquire about the contents?"

"You dare not."

Elaina sniffed the brew. "I choose to be bold."

"Me too." Tawny took a cup.

Elaina dipped her tongue into the mystery liquid. "I'm detecting licorice."

Tawny curled her lips in revulsion. "Not good."

"Sweet red with a splash of vodka and a dash of anise liqueur is a no?"

"A giant nada."

Elaina placed the cup back on the tray. "The combination doesn't rev my engine either."

"Not everyone will like what you make. Tell Nick not to nix the recipe from the cookbook on our account. If you both dig it, keep it." Tawny hollered loud enough for Nick to hear in the kitchen. "Don't use up all the vodka. We have guests coming tomorrow, who may want a slug of hooch with their breakfast." She showed Steph her phone. "Are you familiar with tvorog?"

"It's a type of cottage cheese."

"You knew the Russian word for ham and you know about tvorog. Interesting."

Elaina and Tawny looked at each other, and said, "Spy."

* * *

Elaina held up a sign that read 'Sergei and Alexei'. Expecting tall wrestler-type men who looked like they lived on steroids, she was surprised when two stick-thin gentlemen in their fifties waved from the luggage carousel. She felt foolish for stereotyping; even though it was a common and widespread shortcoming. Some foreigners tagged all Americans as blonde and wealthy. If Sergei and Alexei believed the tag, they were about to get schooled. The four sassy chicks were far from rich. While she had the blonde part down pat, Tawny had light brown hair. Steph was a gorgeous redhead. And Grace's tresses were kept jet black with an occasional streak of purple, thanks to an occasional bottle of dye and hair chalk.

The two men shuffled up to Elaina. One man had reading glasses perched on the end of his nose. "Ride to Sassy Chicks, please."

"Sergei and Alexei?" Of course it was them, but Elaina

didn't know what else to say.

The man said something Elaina wouldn't even attempt to imitate.

"Sergei?"

Sergei smiled and gestured to his traveling companion. "Alexei."

"Nice to meet you. Welcome to Maine." Elaina explained that she'd take them to the bed and breakfast to get checked in, and then they were free to explore Portland.

Dark brows with a weave of silver, dipped down. Sergei handed her his translating device.

Elaina put herself in their shoes. Stepping into a world where you only knew a few words of the language had to be stressful. And if she was set in her ways at the age of forty-four, these gentlemen were probably fixed in theirs as well. Yet here they were, with only a hand-held device to get them through. She typed in the information and showed it to Sergei.

"Rest for while, then walk to discover beautiful city."

On the short drive to the B & B, she listened to them speak to each other in their native tongue. She loved the way they rolled their words.

When she exited I-295, Sergei said "McRib" plain as day. It took a second to comprehend he wanted her to stop at McDonald's. She almost blew by the restaurant. Traffic was light. At the last second, she slammed on the brakes and swung into the parking lot. Elaina swiveled around. "Do you want to go inside to eat or bring your food back to The Four Sassy Chicks?"

Sergei and Alexei tried to interpret what she'd said. They both shrugged. Once again, the translating device was shoved into her hands.

"Eat McRib at a table in the restaurant? Or enjoy it in your room at The Four Sassy Chicks?"

"Eat Four Chicks."

Elaina laughed inwardly.

With their luggage and McRib lunches in hand, Sergei and Alexei looked around the bed and breakfast.

Sergei approved with, "Nice." Alexei said something in Russian.

Elaina showed them to the second floor. She opened one bedroom door and pointed to Sergei. She opened another and directed a finger to Alexei. Body language was universal, thank goodness. She entered the first room and went over the amenities – plenty of towels and toiletries in the bathroom, water and juice in the little fridge, how to find the channel guide on TV, where to find extra blankets and pillows, and she finally handed them the binder with all the location information: taxis, restaurants, attractions, and more. On the back of their door, she touched the laminated sheet with the fire escape plan and route. "Any questions?"

"Set alarm for ferry tomorrow?"

Steph popped into the room, making Alexei flinch. She held out her hand for him to shake. Instead, Alexei kissed it. Steph's green eyes glittered with animation when he touched her hair.

Elaina said the only she could in that odd moment. "Ham."

Chapter Twelve

- Be still, my complicated heart! -

Sergei and Alexei ignored the sausage, snubbed their noses at the fried eggs, and heaped their bowls with oatmeal.

Steph dusted her hands on her apron. "Good thing they didn't ask for tvorog. I looked up the process to make it, and shuddered the entire time. According to the directions, you have to let a gallon of regular milk and a gallon of buttermilk get to room temperature and then pour both into a soup pan. The pan goes into the oven until the milk is lukewarm, which, if you ask me, is redundant. It's already lukewarm from setting on the counter for seven hours. The recipe said to remove the milk from the oven and let it set again, this time for twenty-four hours."

Elaina's gag reflex kicked in and her throat lurched. "You're right, that is disgusting. And I'm fairly certain if I knew how we make cottage cheese, I'd find it just as revolting, and never eat it again."

"Don't hate on cottage cheese." Steph said she'd made it once and proceeded to share the procedure.

Elaina stopped her with a palm in the air. "There's no point. We don't even have a cottage."

"You don't need a cottage to make cottage cheese."

"I know, right?"

Grace shuffled in; her blue eyes alight with something indefinable. "You're not going to believe what I'm about to say."

"You won the lottery," Tawny said nonsensically.

"You have to actually play the lottery to win, which I don't."

Elaina teased with a silly guess. "You found out you have foot fungus."

"Eww! No!"

Steph popped a purple grape in her mouth. "You were named Bowling Champion of the Year."

"You goofball. The last time I bowled was that Sunday in Cherry Ridge when Tawny coached you to aim for the head pin, only she said G-spot instead. I thought the women bowling next to us were going to pee their pants, they laughed so hard."

"We had a blast that day."

Elaina sprinkled half a grapefruit with salt. "You didn't win the lottery. You say your feet are fungus-free. And there's zero chance that you're Bowling Champion of the Year. There's only one thing left – Brad Pitt followed you on Twitter."

"I wish."

"A thousand guesses and we'd still be wrong, so just

tell us, Grace." Steph cut a pancake in fourths, and wrapped sausage links in each piece – a technique she used these days to cut carbs.

"You're no fun."

"Fun is in there." Steph inclined her head toward the dining room. "The guy from Idaho stunned us all this morning by speaking flawless Russian to Sergei and Alexei. Let your mind entertain that for a moment."

The pitch of Grace's voice was suddenly heavy with suspicion. "That might explain why Officer Chad Ferguson is parked out front."

Elaina stilled. Grace had no logical reason for making something like that up. It had to be true. Chad Ferguson was in Portland, and had come to the bed and breakfast. Nervous curiosity took over Elaina. She tried to disguise it with a façade of indifference. "Sure he is."

"I'm not trying to get a rise out of you. Chad is, in fact, outside. He brought his own car, not a police cruiser."

"Well duh," Tawny clipped. "That would be a dead giveaway to the bad guys he wants to apprehend."

Elaina stated that Chad was now part of an elite detective unit that tracked down those sent to cause mayhem in our country.

"Elaina Samuels, I'm glad you're just as suspicious as me and Grace."

"I'm observant when it comes to our guests. It isn't the same as being suspicious."

The doorbell rang. Philip let Chad in and gave him an enthusiastic welcome. "Chad Ferguson! How the heck are you?"

Steph and Tawny turned to leave the kitchen. Elaina thrust out an arm to barricade their departure. "Don't go."

With a slow, sly smile, Tawny asked why she should stay.

"You know why." Elaina wrung her hands. "I can't look. Is he in uniform?"

Like a secret agent, Tawny peered around the doorway, and then ducked back in. "He is not. He's...wait for it, wait for it," she said a second time. "He's stark naked."

Elaina blasted Tawny with a slit-eyed frown. "Don't do that to me."

"I love this reaction. Are you digging the effect he's having on her, Grace?"

"I can't get enough of it."

"Scale back the wisecracks, please," Elaina commanded.

Tawny moved out of striking range. "Steph, are you seeing what we're seeing?"

Steph concurred by constantly nodding. "I'm seeing it, Tawn'."

"I just...I don't..."

Tawny slung an arm around Elaina. "It's good to see you flustered about a man."

"I'm not flustered. I'm trying to process his presence. Your guess could be accurate. He could be here to unravel a spy network."

Tawny scoffed. "What your little heart refuses to consider is that he might be here for you."

"You're so not funny." Elaina swayed to the right to

glimpse Chad. She watched him make over Stony. That was a huge surprise. One of the last times they were together, Chad exhibited jealousy regarding the dog.

Stony seemed happy to see Chad. He offered up his famous yowl and jumped to place his paws on Chad's chest.

Elaina heard Chad say he missed Stony. Bailey didn't want Stony getting all the attention. She weaved in and out of Chad's legs. "Who's your mini-me, Stone-man?" He picked up Bailey, and the tiny dog licked his face.

Holy mother of pearl! What was happening?

Tawny brought Elaina back to the conversation. "How do you think it will go down?"

"If Chad is here on official business, he won't let on. He'll act like we're long, lost friends, while surveying the scene."

"That's some great confidence coming from a woman he used to date. Remind me again why you broke up?"

Steph provided the details. "Their stars didn't align."

"Planets align, stars do not," Tawny stated, like she knew everything about the solar system.

"Ert! You're wrong; well, kind of wrong. Did you know the major planets never perfectly align? The last time they came close was eons ago and it won't happen again until the year 2492." Grace clicked her tongue.

"There she goes again with the 'Did you know stuff'."

Philip escorted Chad to the kitchen. "Elaina, Chad would like to have a few words with you in private."

Elaina swallowed hard to clear a sudden clog in her throat. "Nice to see you, Chad."

"Good to see you too, Elaina." His deep-green eyes latched onto hers and wouldn't let go.

Elaina suggested they step into the living room.

Chad proposed a different location. "How about the basement?"

Elaina kept her eyes fixed on Chad, even though she desperately wanted to gain support with a look at Tawny. "Sure."

Tucked away from prying eyes, Chad came inches from Elaina. He was so close she could smell an earthy-cologne on his skin and a hint of peppermint on his breath.

"How are things in New York City?"

"Exciting. Diverse. Crowded."

"And you came back to Portland to get the rest of your belongings?" Elaina skimmed her eyes across his mouth and felt a strange pang in her belly.

"I actually brought some things back to Portland."

"Did you accidentally take things that belonged to someone else?"

"That wasn't the case." Chad boldly placed his hands on her hips.

Elaina inhaled a sharp breath.

Chad dropped his hands and inched back.

Elaina smiled and returned his hands.

"For a lot of years, I thought the Big Apple was where I wanted to be. I craved the intensity and chaos of a big city. Once I got a taste, I realized it didn't give me the satisfaction that I thought it would. There were a number of other reasons why I wanted to move back home. You're one of them."

Elaina's mouth unhinged at the jaw.

Chad brushed his thumb across her bottom lip.

A shiver of delight coursed through Elaina.

In a spontaneous and shocking move, he claimed her mouth with a fiery kiss.

When they parted, Elaina panted to get her uneven breathing back in line. Chad did the same.

They stared at each other for at least a dozen blinks.

"I don't know what to say."

"Say you'll let me back in." He sighed. "I shouldn't have left in the first place."

"You had to go. It was your dream to be there."

"My captain put in a good word for me with a friend he had in the NYPD. That was shortly after you and I met. I knew there was a good chance I'd be leaving Portland for the Big Apple, so I purposely didn't let you and I get too cozy – even though I was crazy about you. I got the job offer, and things started to change up here." He tapped his head. "I wanted to give the Big Apple all of me, but I had a struggle going on inside of me. The thing I wanted more than anything in the world was finally going to happen, yet my thoughts were all over the place. I convinced myself that as soon as I got to New York, my feelings would settle down."

"They didn't?"

"I tried to force them to. It didn't work. I became impatient and tense. I finally asked for a meeting with my lieutenant."

"What did he say?"

Chad worked his hands through Elaina's hair. "He

said, 'Who is she?'"

Elaina's lashes flew up.

"I'm sure my face showed as much surprise as yours does now." He continued to play with her hair. "Don't take this wrong, but I denied my lieutenant's theory...at least to him."

"Chad, please don't say you walked away from something you've wanted forever, because of me.

"After I left the lieutenant's office, I had a heart-to-heart talk with myself and came to the conclusion I'd be more effective in a city the size of Portland. I realized I didn't want the nonstop uproar that comes with major urban sprawl, after all. That's not saying Portland doesn't have problems; every city does. The only nonstop uproar I want is the kind stirred by your blue eyes. Neither of us can deny the physical attraction between us. You know it's there. I know it's there. But we have more than chemistry. We share a love for running, yoga, healthy eating, and the state of Maine. I could go on and on."

"Chad, I..."

He put their foreheads together. "Don't break my heart by telling me you want nothing to do with me."

"I did not see this coming and I'm trying to process what you're saying." She took a half-step back. "You pushed me away."

"Which I regret."

"My confidence took a hit. I questioned everything about myself, especially why I couldn't keep a man's attention. Arden tossed me aside. Michael and I had a good relationship for a while. The first time I laid eyes on you, I felt a special pull. Then New York City happened. You left, and I was a complete and utter mess. I hid the crack in my heart and led my friends to believe I was fine. To heighten the illusion – not only to them, but to myself – I did something really stupid."

"Burned my picture in effigy?"

"Nothing quite so bizarre." Elaina shifted from foot to foot. "We had a guest. A musician."

Chad inhaled a significant breath. "You married him?"

"What? No! I'm not that batty." Elaina dropped her head.

"I need to see your eyes." Chad raised her chin.

"Jess made it plain he wasn't ready for a relationship. Despite his warning that there'd be no long-term connection for us, my distorted sense-of-self still went gaga over him. I thought I was in love. He moved to Virginia and I sulked for longer than I ever have in my life."

"Are you saying your heart belongs to Jess?"

"No. He doesn't own it."

"How can you be sure?"

"Kiss me again and we'll both know."

Slowly, seductively, Chad took Elaina's face in his hands. Keeping their gazes intact, he kissed her first with his eyes, and then descended on her mouth. His gentle caress of her lips quickly turned into heavy hunger. Spirals of ecstasy tried to buckle Elaina's knees. She had to lean into him to remain upright.

Stopping just long enough to catch his breath, Chad

devoured her again. Then he moved from her mouth to the pulsing hollow of her throat and placed tender kisses against her skin.

They jumped apart at the sound of the basement door being opened.

"I hate to be a buttinski," Grace hollered, "but Sergei keeps asking for you."

Elaina kept her eyes linked with Chad's and informed Grace that she'd be upstairs in a little bit. When they were alone again, she put a hand on Chad's chest and found his heart thumping wildly against his ribs. "Yowza!"

Chad touched her lips with his fingers.

"All..." Elaina started again, this time with more conviction. "All uncertainty has been erased."

A tender smile tugged up the corners of Chad's mouth. "I have no doubt that I made the right choice, Elaina." He drew her close and massaged her lower back. "I'm not sure I can compete with a rock star though."

"Jess isn't a rock star. He composes music for them. He reeled me in with a song."

"What song?"

Elaina buried her face in Chad's neck.

"Let's get it all out in the open."

"*A Little Bit More* by Dr. Hook."

"Wow. That is a great song. How can a woman not lose her mind with romantic lyrics like those? I'd lose my mind over them too." There wasn't a trace of mocking in his tone.

"Forget Jess. Forget the song. You craved intensity and chaos. In a way, so did I; just differently. Mine included having my head in the clouds for a while. That won't happen again."

"Does that mean we'll have fun together, but your heart is off-limits?"

"Nothing of the sort, Officer Ferguson. I'm trying to tell you I'm no longer a hot mess. I'm glad you're here. And the only reason I told you about Jess is so you know how your leaving for New York affected me, and what took place in your absence."

Chad pecked the tip of her nose with a soft kiss. "I'm not thrilled to hear about you and Jess. However, I'm glad that *you're glad* I'm here. It gives me hope." He tucked a strand of hair behind Elaina's ear. "Portland P.D. has agreed to put me back on their roster. Will you do the same?"

"I don't have a roster of men." She paused to change and choose her words carefully. "I'd be happy to let you back in my life, on one condition."

"Anything. Name it."

"We take things slowly and become good friends before we become lovers."

"What about the physical attraction? It's phenomenal! And it's hot! I see it in your eyes and I tasted it in your kiss."

"It's there all right, burning me up inside. It'll be difficult to hold off." Elaina traced his jaw line with her index finger. "We can kiss, hold hands, hug, touch..." She purposely left the thought unfinished.

"But no bedroom activity."

"I want to know everything about you. Mostly, I don't

want my heart to take another leap without the feeling being mutual."

"Elaina Ashlynn Samuels, you're beautiful and brilliant, and my racing pulse is about to blow every vein in my body."

"And you're devastatingly handsome. That's why I have to be careful. My eyes like what I see. I can't let them be the boss." She played with the collar of his shirt. "You remembered my middle name."

"The details of the day you arrived in Portland are still etched in my mind. I made you produce documentation that you owned the bed and breakfast. Your full name came up."

Elaina's heart did a somersault. "Did I mention I'm glad you're here?" She chuckled. "Speaking of diverse, there's a man from Russia in need of my attention."

* * *

"More eggs, Chaddy-boy?"

Chad made a face at the nickname. "No thank you."

As soon as they went back upstairs, Tawny had looped an arm through Chad's. She dragged him to the table and insisted he have breakfast. He'd eaten a few bites of eggs, nothing more.

The guest from Idaho, who'd easily conversed with Sergei and Alexei, zipped his eyes back and forth from Elaina to Chad several times. "Tawny's been trying to make me eat more eggs and bacon too."

Sergei's eyes bored a hole through Elaina. "America,

fine place."

"Thank you, Sergei."

From her peripheral, Elaina watched Chad watch her guests. He was doing exactly what Grace and Tawny wanted him to do – putting his gut instinct and police skills to good use.

"Taxi, no." Sergei pointed to Elaina. "Pay you to take us to ferry?"

Of course, that's why Sergei wanted to talk to her.

Grace started to explain that they transported guests to and from the airport, not to other sites. Elaina stopped Grace with a bump of her shoe.

"I'd be happy to take you." It wasn't the first time Elaina had broken protocol, and it probably wouldn't be the last.

Chad offered to ride along.

To protect her? "That would be great. I've never been to where the ferries launch. You can show me the way." Elaina placed a hand on Chad's thigh, but removed it right away. *Friends first.* She had to keep that in mind.

"You deserve a cinnamon roll." Tawny shoved the plate loaded with rolls to him. "Did I mention how amazing you are?"

There was a twinkle of amusement in Chad's eyes from Tawny's sucking up. He gave Elaina a knowing smile.

"She's not wrong." Elaina dropped walnuts and pumpkins seeds into a cup of peach yogurt.

Steph cut Tawny with a look of annoyance. "Grady left an hour ago and you're already hitting on Chad."

In rebuttal, Tawny stuck her tongue out. "I'm not flirting with Chad. I'm thanking him for..." She swung a question to Elaina. "What exactly am I thanking him for?"

Elaina issued Tawny an order to behave.

Chad laughed.

"Now I remember. I'm thanking him for making you happy. Just look at you – you're glowing."

Elaina rolled her eyes.

Chad took Elaina's hand. "It's good to see you glowing."

"I know, right?"

He moved his knee touch Elaina's. "As soon as we get back from dropping your friends off at the ferry, I'm going to go for a run. I haven't done that in ages."

Sergei perked in an instant. "Running, I like."

Elaina stirred her yogurt. "What time do you board the ferry?"

Sergei held up two fingers.

"Two o'clock. Got it. We have time to run beforehand. Would you like to run with Chad and me?"

Chad appeared surprised. "You'll run with me?"

"We share a love for fitness, remember?"

"I didn't consider that you could leave." He whispered so only she could hear, "We also share a love for kissing."

Every nerve-ending in Elaina's body came alive.

"I'd ask what you two are all hush-hush about, but I think I know." Tawny did a fist-pump. "Finally!"

With just a look, Elaina told Tawny to butt out.

Chad extended Elaina's offer to Sergei again. "Would you and Alexei care to run with us?"

"Sergei wants shower. American TV we watch."

Chad nodded.

"Tawny and Steph, will you take care of the breakfast clutter? Chad and I will be in the fitness room, warming up."

"You're actually going to run?"

Chad answered for them both, "We are."

"Outside?"

"There's not enough room on the treadmill for two, so...."

"Elaina, before you get all sweaty with Chad, can I borrow you for a minute?"

* * *

Elaina was tugged into Tawny's bedroom. "I get the feeling you're going to do to me what I usually do to you – get all Mother Hen-ish."

"Bak. Bak." Tawny's humor faded. "I assume things went well with Chad."

Elaina sat on the edge of the bed. "Better than expected."

A long, cavernous sigh, that sounded as though it had been repressed for months, rolled out of Tawny. "Thank the Lord! It's about time."

"He's moving back to Portland."

"I knew it! I could tell by the look in his eyes something great was about to take place."

"The jury is out on the greatness of this unexpected development."

Tawny sat beside Elaina. "I tease you a lot, but what

I'm about to say is a hundred-percent tease-free." She shifted to look Elaina in the eye. "This is straight from the heart too." She shared her feelings about Arden, Michael, Chad, and Jess. "Chad has been my favorite all along. I'll admit I was pissed at him when he moved away. I didn't say much on the subject, because I didn't want to upset you further." Tawny scratched her head. "Although," she paused, "if I remember correctly, you weren't too torn up when he left."

"I was torn up. I just didn't want him or anyone else to know."

"And now?"

"Things are good and I can't stop smiling."

What Tawny said next jolted Elaina. "I hope you're so stinking happy with each other that you walk down the aisle soon."

"Whoa! Pump the brakes! Better yet, slam them to the floorboard and stop that crazy talk." To further drive home her point, Elaina checked her radial pulse. "My blood pressure is going haywire."

"Not because of me, because of Chad."

"You're getting squirrely, Tawn'. You should probably take a nap."

"Ha." Tawny blew off Elaina's attempt to downplay the Chad-effect. "You want him. Go ahead, say it."

Elaina lowered her lashes until her eyes were almost closed.

"You have this annoying habit of over-thinking and dissecting everything. You constantly tell us to follow our hearts, but never take your own advice. Listen, woman, embrace the cliché about letting down your guard. You had eyes for Jess, but I never saw them shine quite like they do when you look at Chad."

"That's not shine. It's a glob of mascara."

"When you try to be funny, it seldom works." Tawny expelled a heavy breath of air. "While my opinion seems to be wild, it isn't. It's designed especially for you at this moment. Don't dawdle with Chad. Give it all to him, not just a speck at a time."

"That's not me, Tawn'."

"Let it be you."

"I lose my way when I go fast."

"You could lose Chad if you go at a snail's pace."

Tawny meant well. But there was no way Elaina could zoom through all the relevant things in a relationship; like getting to know one another's likes and dislikes, strengths and weaknesses, idiosyncrasies and remarkable traits, and making sweet memories that can only come from being with a person from courtship to old age. Bottom line: she wanted to take things one day at a time and see where it took them. "If I don't move fast enough to suit him, then he's not for me."

"The only way to get something through that thick skull of yours is with a drill." Tawny's cell phone plinked. "Grady made it to JFK. He says he misses me already." She typed something and tossed her phone on the bed.

The phone plinked again.

"I'll leave you two alone."

* * *

Elaina intended to join Chad in the fitness room. Nick flew down the stairs and grabbed her arm, his eyes darting in every direction. "I need to talk to you while Steph vacuums."

"Ohhh-kay."

Nick hurried her toward the kitchen. Stony ambled to the center of the room and got in their way. At the last second, Nick tried to avoid a collision. He caught the tip of Stony's paw with his shoe.

Stony whimpered.

Nick released Elaina and stooped to check Stony's foot. "I didn't mean to hurt you, boy." He warmed Elaina's heart when he planted a kiss on Stony's nose. "My size thirteen clodhoppers get in the way all the time."

Stony brushed against Nick.

"I think you're forgiven."

"Thanks, Stone-man." Nick shot a look up the stairway. "We have to be quick." As soon as they were in the kitchen, he checked again to make sure they were alone. "Could I see the reservation ledger?"

"You don't have to ask. You can check it out anytime you want."

"I prefer to have you present."

"Are you going to surprise Steph with a trip?"

A big grin replaced his seriousness. "I'm going to try." Nick flipped pages back and forth. He studied two pages in particular. "I have a huge favor to ask."

"Shoot."

"What do you think about me whisking Steph away the second week in May? You have a few reservations, but...."

"Does this trip have special significance?'

Nick tramped to the doorway to verify the coast was still clear. He spoke so quietly that Elaina had to strain to hear him. "Our cookbook is finally finished. Well, we have to finish the cover art and then it will be complete."

"I thought your cover was done months ago."

"It needs some tweaking."

"Don't you like the picture of you and Steph on the front?"

"I love that picture."

"Then what?"

Nick had whispering down to a fine art. He said something and Elaina had to ask him to repeat it. "Steph's excited and can't wait for it to be published. I'm just as eager, although I don't want it to hit the stores until the cover says Stephanie and Nicholas Augustine, instead of Stephanie Mathews and Nicholas Augustine."

"You want to marry Steph ahead of publication."

"The cookbook is the driving force for the rush, but the truth is, I can't wait for Steph to be my wife."

"That is so great, Nick."

"Do you think she'll go for tying the knot this soon?"

The hurry-up-and-get-hitched syndrome seemed to be the theme of the day – or a serious illness. The ledger lay open to May fourteenth. "It's the best birthday gift a girl could get."

Could life get crazier? As soon as the question filtered

through Elaina's thoughts, the answer came from Grace.

"There you are. I found Chad stretching his hammies, without you."

"I was unavoidably detained." Elaina wouldn't nark out Nick, who'd cleverly stuck his head in the refrigerator to throw Grace off.

"Sergei enjoys hogging you. He seems comfortable with you."

"I took them through McDonald's for McRib sandwiches. Who wouldn't like me after that heroic effort?" Elaina threw her hair over her shoulder to heighten the theatrics.

"Whatever."

"Found it." Nick came out of the refrigerator with a package of blue cheese. "A steak salad with blue cheese crumbles would hit the spot."

"We just had breakfast," Grace exclaimed.

"I meant for lunch or dinner." Nick stuffed the cheese back in the fridge. "I'm a foodie. When I'm not thinking about sex, I'm thinking about food."

Grace stuck her fingers in her ears. "La La La."

Nick chortled and removed himself from the kitchen.

Elaina pulled Grace's finger away. "He's Steph in a man's body."

Instead of agreeing, Grace walked to the window and looked out.

Elaina had yet to make it to Chad. "Did you need to talk to me about something?"

In an abrupt and surprise move, Grace threw her arms around Elaina.

"Thank you for the hug, although I'm not sure what I did to earn it. Or are you laying groundwork?"

Nothing from Grace, not even a blink.

"Out with it. Anytime now, Chad will be ready to run and I don't want to hold him up."

In another unexpected shift, Grace's eyes watered. "When I went upstairs, I noticed I had a missed Facetime call from Cody. I called him back."

"Are you crying because Facetime kept dropping out?"

The question prompted Grace to respond with a lengthy, "Noooo."

"Is everything okay with the baby?"

Grace threw herself into Elaina again and held on tight. "Everything's perfect. Absolutely perfect. They Facetime'd to tell me they're having a boy and they've picked out a name."

Emotion also hit Elaina's eyes, when she put two and two together. "They're going to name him Brince."

"My heart is overflowing with happiness!" Grace laid her head on Elaina's chest.

"Cody has given you a great gift. And I believe Brince is doing a happy dance in Heaven."

Chad walked into the kitchen. His eyes rounded with surprise.

Elaina smiled warmly.

He blew her a kiss and backed out of the room.

Tawny, however, didn't pay close attention. She barreled in, grabbed an apple from the bowl on the counter, and plopped down in a chair. "What the....?"

Grace pulled away from Elaina and typed something

into her phone.

"What's with the waterworks?"

Grace grabbed a tissue and dabbed at her eyes. "I can't say just yet."

"Why not? Does Elaina know?"

Grace took another tissue and blew her nose.

Elaina tried to keep a blank expression so she wouldn't give anything away.

Philip burst through the front door and ran to them out of breath. "I came as fast as these spindly legs would carry me." His eyes dropped to the tissue in Grace's hand and then lowered his gaze even farther to her feet. "Did you sprain your ankle again?"

"I'm not hurt."

Steph and Nick crowded the doorway, and Chad was suddenly there too.

Nick hawk-eyed Elaina. "Please tell me you didn't spill the beans."

Steph cocked her head in confusion. "What beans?"

Elaina subtly pointed to Grace.

Grace took Philip's hand. "We're having a boy!"

Tawny tried to get up in a hurry and knocked the chair sideways. "The baby has a bobber?"

Philip picked up Grace. "Congratulations, sweetheart!" He put her down and held her to his chest. "Thank you for allowing me to be part of your family."

A flurry of joy filled the kitchen.

"That's incredible news, Grace Vivian. We have to celebrate." Steph picked out a bottle of sparkling wine from the rack and grabbed the corkscrew.

"We'll possibly be celebrating two things," Nick announced.

Steph swiveled around with curiosity and the corkscrew.

Tawny jumped to conclusions. "You and Steph are having a baby too?"

Nick kept his eyes glued to Steph's. "Not that I'm aware of." He removed the corkscrew from her hand. "I have to get this said or I'll explode."

"What is it, Nick?" Steph softly inquired.

Nick brought her hand to his lips. "You're still getting used to the idea of marrying me, I know, but I want to run something by you. Besides eating red velvet birthday cake with cream cheese frosting on May fourteenth, would you also consider saying the words 'I do'?"

Steph was rendered speechless.

"If you have your heart set on a big wedding, we can wait." Nick placed his mouth close to Steph's ear and whispered something

Elaina didn't try to home in on the personal exchange, but Nick's inflection on the word cookbook was hard to miss.

"I'd marry you this second, Nicholas Augustine, if I could." Steph moved a lock of hair across his forehead. "Give me a big kitchen and a small wedding, and I'll be ecstatic."

"Done!"

Steph smiled up at him. "All we really need is each other, our families, best friends, and a priest."

"So that's a yes?"

Steph shouted an exuberant, "Yes!"

Chapter Thirteen

- Things are piling up! -

Chad handed Elaina her coat. "Could I talk to you alone for a few minutes?"

"Where are we headed?"

"It's safe to say outside." Tawny flicked Elaina on the wrist when she walked past. "Remember, go fast."

In the breezeway, Chad asked what Tawny had meant.

"She thinks I should pick out a china pattern."

Chad's eyebrows pinched together. "Why?"

Elaina squirmed under his intense gaze. "Because she's a lovable lunatic."

"I'm still not getting a clear picture."

"Picking out china means...."

"No, I got that part."

Elaina's laugh contained very little mirth. "My harebrained friend thinks you and I should skip dating and go straight to the church for vows."

Caught off guard, Chad drew back like she'd taken a swat at him. "No kidding?"

Elaina had a feeling he'd said something a little stronger in his mind. "I should explain where she's coming from. Grace and Philip are on the fast-track to get married, even though Philip has yet to propose. As you witnessed, Steph and Nick are headed to the altar in May. I'm sure when Grady gets things taken care of in Ohio, he and Tawny will re-tie the knot. Tawny's worried that I'll be lonely. What she doesn't understand is that being alone doesn't necessarily mean lonely. I'll be fine."

"She's a good friend."

"The four of us are sisters of the heart. We look out for each other."

They walked to the stone bench that circled the fire pit.

"You won't be alone, I promise."

Elaina blinked up at him. "We're new together, Chad. Newbies don't make promises."

"Are newbies allowed to do this?"

He kissed her like they were lovers who'd been separated for years. He deepened the mouth-to-mouth action until they either had to come up for air or pass out.

They bent at the waist and sucked air to refill their lungs. Between gulps, they smiled.

Straightening, Chad lessened the space between them. With Elaina close once again, he traced the outline of her jaw with his thumb. "It might not be too soon to pick out china, after all."

"Call me conservative, but I need to know a few things before I choose dishes for the table."

"Such as?"

Elaina decided to keep things light. "Do you snore?"

"Yes."

"Honesty. I like it." Sunlight hit his green eyes and Elaina thought she'd melt. "Question number two: morning person or night owl?"

"Definitely morning. It comes from being a cop. I've always worked the day shift."

Elaina moved her finger over the cleft in his chin. "What are some things you've done, that I most likely haven't?"

"I could name a hundred things."

"Name two."

"Hang-gliding and zip-lining."

"I can't see myself hang-gliding, but I wouldn't mind giving zip-lining a try."

"Let's do it, preferably in the summer. The forest is too wet right now." He massaged her rhomboid muscles. "Next question."

"What wrong assumptions do people make about you?"

Chad came up with an answer without having to dig deep. "Because I'm into exercise and take extra-care with my appearance, I've been called conceited. I'm okay with it though. They can think whatever they like."

"You're not conceited."

"Thank you."

"You're welcome. On to some serious questions. What's your biggest fear, not job-related?"

Chad looked up at the sky. "Losing someone I love."

Elaina snuggled into him. "Good answer."

He pecked her mouth with a tender kiss. "Continue the interrogation."

She shifted in his arms. "If your best guy friend was having a difficult day and needed to talk, but you had a prior commitment with the woman you really cared for and didn't want to tick her off, what would you do?"

"Are you trying to trick me?"

Elaina laughed. "Just answer the question, Officer Ferguson."

"Hands down, I'd make time for my buddy. If the woman didn't understand why I had to break the date, she's not a keeper."

"You get an A."

"I passed the test?"

"The first one."

"There's more?"

"Don't worry – I'll space out the exams."

"Good thing. I'd hate to flunk out on the first day."

"Do you have questions for me?"

Chad played with a strand of her hair. "A few. In the past, we didn't go out a lot. We spent most of our time with your friends. This time around I'd occasionally like to have you to myself. Would that be okay?"

"Works for me."

"Second question: can I steal you away tomorrow night for lobster rolls and crab?"

"My mouth just watered."

"Mine too." He stared at her mouth and dove in for another searing kiss.

"You also get an A for knowing how to turn my legs to jelly."

"Glad I'm improving, I got B's in school."

They laughed together.

"With tourist season almost here, I won't delude myself into thinking you're available 24/7. But I'd really like to take you to Cadillac Mountain some morning to watch the sunrise. Will you pencil me in?"

"It's a date."

"Ms. Samuels, you're passing with flying colors too."

Elaina pulled at his ear lobe. "I didn't study for the test ahead of time, I swear."

He snickered. "I love your sense of humor."

"According to the girls, my humor needs some fine-tuning."

Chad looked toward the house. "We're being watched."

Expecting Tawny, Steph, and Grace to have their noses smashed against the window, Elaina was surprised to see Philip hawk-eyeing them. "He wouldn't be staring unless he had a good reason." She waved.

Philip opened the door and held up a phone. "Chad, this thing has been ringing like crazy. I thought you should know."

"I'll be right there. Thanks, Philip." Chad grasped Elaina's hand. "This session of getting-to-know-you has to come to a close. I've only been back for a day, so I'm not scheduled to work until Monday. But I volunteered to be on-call. The boys in blue must need my help."

Reaching the door, Elaina said she had one more question.

Chad had already flipped into work-mode. He shifted from foot to foot, ready to get on the move. "Okay."

"Do you have a place to stay?"

"A buddy is lending me his couch until I find an apartment."

She angled her head to the backyard. "Would you like to rent the loft apartment? It comes with privacy and breakfast."

Chad stopped fidgeting. "Consider it rented."

Elaina felt giddy inside. "Excellent. I'll get you a key."

"You wouldn't feel like I'm in your space too much?"

"Not at all. You have work to do and so do I. When time permits, we'll sneak a kiss." She also let him know that if things didn't work out between them, she'd treat him like she treated the other guests – with kindness and respect.

"Things are going to work out, Elaina. I'm determined not to mess things up again."

* * *

Elaina threw wet towels into the dryer and dialed the setting to hot. She rested against the washer and began to process the day. Chad had come back into her life. As hard as her subconscious resisted the idea, her heart had more strength, and they were now an official couple.

She thought about Sergei and Alexei. Their sweet personalities had shown her that people were the same the world over. They didn't want their government's politics to follow them around; they wanted friendship and acceptance. At the boat ferry, Sergei had kissed her cheek. Alexei had remained aloof, but that was okay – she hadn't expected him to suddenly break out of his shell. Then there was Nick and Steph setting a wedding date. There were a ton of things to do, even though they opted to have a small wedding. She'd offered to help with whatever they needed.

"I wondered where you got off to." Grace entered the utility room with what appeared to be funky looking smoothies. She kicked the door closed with her foot.

"I thought I'd catch up on laundry." Elaina took one of the glasses. "What is this?"

"A blend of frozen strawberries, beetroot, spinach, coconut milk, and a slew of other stuff from the fridge that Steph decided to use up."

Elaina sampled the drink. "It tastes better than it looks." She set it on the washer and stored the bottle of fabric softener in the overhead cabinet.

"You're not in here to catch up on laundry."

"I'm not?" Elaina tapped the dryer. "It seems like I am."

"I know you like the back of my hand. You're trying to make sense of a crazy day." Grace perched beside Elaina. "I'm right there with you."

"Grandma Grace is going to have a grandson."

Grace's smile was priceless. "I'm overwhelmed and feel blessed at the same time."

"Why are you overwhelmed?"

Grace fluttered her eyes closed.

"Does this have to do with Brince?"

A small sob worked its way up and out of Grace. She opened her eyes and shrugged. "I thought I'd dealt with all these feelings when I first found out Isabella was pregnant."

"As it turns out, you have a few left to take care of."

"Elaina, I have to talk to Brince." Grace swallowed hard. "Would you go with me to Ohio? It's a lot to ask, especially with Steph's wedding day fast approaching."

Elaina didn't hesitate. "Care to take a red-eye? I can be ready in five minutes." She snatched the smoothie and motioned for Grace to follow her. In the living room, she found Tawny and Steph relaxing in recliners. "Grace and I are taking a trip. Want to come along?"

Tawny put the footrest of the recliner down. "Road trip?"

"It's more of a sky trip. We'll be in a plane."

"Where are you headed?"

"Cherry Ridge, to visit Brince."

"I'm in. Are you in, Steph?"

Steph moaned. "I want to go, but it hinges on how long we'll be gone."

Elaina let Grace provide the details.

"We'll catch a plane tonight and be back before midnight tomorrow."

Steph pulled at her bottom lip with her teeth. "Could we stop at the bridal shop on Wayne Street?"

"We'll make time for it."

Tawny also had a request. "Can we drop in to see Grady?"

Grace nodded. "I'm sure he'd be upset if we didn't."

Elaina rubbed her hands together. "While we're in

Ohio, I'd like for us to make a special stop; actually, two special stops."

Tawny squinched her eyes together. "Please don't say you want to visit Arden. I may upchuck, if you do."

"I've seen enough of Arden to last me for years."

"What are the special stops?"

"You'll find out after we visit Brince, the bridal store, and Grady." Elaina headed toward the basement. "Let's do this. Throw a toothbrush and a pair of underwear in your purse, and then we'll head to the airport."

"Thank you. I need this more than you know."

"So do we, Grace."

Steph paused at the stairway. "Is the underwear in case our return flight gets cancelled? We can't get grounded. I have too many things to do."

"Don't panic, Steph. Everything will turn out okay." At least Elaina hoped they would. It was springtime. This time of year, the weather goddess was moody. She was known to snap her fingers and change a sunny day into something that delayed aircraft for hours."

Elaina and Steph hadn't even made it to their rooms, and Tawny was back in a flash.

"I brought two pair of underwear, just in case."

Steph put a hand on her forehead. "So much to do. So much to do."

With a bossy tone, Tawny told Steph to snap out of it or stay home.

"I'm not staying home. Grace might sprain another ankle and I'm not missing it this time." Steph ascended the steps two at a time.

"What does Nick see in her?" Tawny asked, loud enough for Steph to hear.

Nick appeared at the banister. "The same things you see in her."

"Weird behavior?"

Steph shot out of her bedroom with a pillow. She hurled it at Tawny with all her might, but missed her mark.

Elaina crossed her arms. "We don't have time for a pillow fight."

"Wanna bet?" Tawny snatched up the pillow and walloped Elaina aside of the head.

Chapter Fourteen

~ No Sweat Pants Allowed — Wine Club! ~

At five o'clock in the morning, the airplane touched down in Dayton.

As they walked through the terminal to reach the rental car desk, Steph searched her purse for a mint. In the process, her extra pair of underwear fell on the tiled floor of the terminal. She stared at them wide-eyed and then walked away.

One of the passengers from their flight shouted from behind them. "Hey, you dropped something."

Steph mumbled under her breath, "Walk faster."

The guy caught up with her. "Ma'am, you lost these."

"No I didn't."

Elaina pressed her lips together to keep from laughing.

It finally dawned on the Good Samaritan why Steph refused to acknowledge ownership. "You're embarrassed."

Grace held her hand out to take the underwear. "I'd be embarrassed too, if my bloomers were decorated with lizards."

Steph's response was quick and loud. "They're geckos."

The guy innocently pointed out, "Geckos are lizards."

Steph frowned.

"Booyah!" Tawny put her hand up for him to high-five.

Elaina thanked the guy for his good deed and handed him a twenty-dollar bill. "Have a cup of coffee on us."

He waved away the money. "I appreciate the gesture. Buy her a cup of coffee instead. She needs it more than I do."

Steph snatched the bill from Elaina and thrust it at him. "I'm so sorry. You did this kind thing and I practically bit your head off."

"No you didn't. You tried to hide from the undies. I would've done the same thing." He grinned. "You gals take care."

Steph whimpered after he left. "I'm grouchy from lack of sleep."

"Nah. It's a case of nerves and a lack of caffeine. One we can fix. The other you'll have to work through."

By daylight, they'd made it to Cherry Ridge.

At the first traffic light, Elaina asked, "Breakfast first?"

Grace sat in the front seat with her head down. Without looking up, she said, "Yes, please."

Tawny recommended Ziggy's – the mom and pop diner on South Pierce Street. "They opened at six."

"Good suggestion, Tawn'. I have another idea." Elaina drove until they came to a familiar restaurant.

Grace gasped. "I can't thank you enough for this."

"It's all good. Now get your butt out of the car."

They stretched to work out the kinks of the plane

ride, and the hour and a half car ride.

Elaina linked arms with Grace. "Are you ready for combo number five?"

Tawny began to gyrate and sing Lou Bega's song.

Steph gave her thumbs-down. "It's combo number five, not *Mambo No. 5*. Combo number five includes eggs-over-easy, blueberry pancakes, bacon, sausage, and home fries."

Elaina was dumbfounded. "How in the world did you remember that?"

Steph lifted her shoulders in a shrug. "I recall being shocked when they brought out all that food and set it in front of Grace. And then Grace said this was Brince's favorite restaurant and that he always ordered the lumberjack plate. It was a touching moment and somehow the items on the plate embedded themselves in my brain."

Grace squeezed Steph's hand. "You amaze me, Steph."

"Back at ya, Grace."

An hour later, they arrived at Shady Oaks Cemetery and drove through the maze of stone streets until Grace pumped her palm for Elaina to stop the car.

"Do you want us to stay here?" The last time they'd come to the cemetery, Grace had wanted privacy to talk to Brince.

"Come with me. I need all of your support to get through this."

They followed in silence.

Almost there, Grace asked for just a minute with him alone.

Grace dropped to her knees at Brince's grave, even though the ground was soggy. They couldn't hear her words, but they could see her tears.

It was a powerful scene. Elaina started to cry too. Tawny and Steph didn't hold back their emotions either.

Grace summoned them.

Through a river of tears, Grace began. "Brince, I'm okay – my friends Elaina, Tawny, and Steph are with me. I wish you could meet them. They'd make you laugh. They're the best."

It might've been ten minutes before she spoke again.

"Cody and I miss you so much. Some nights I cry myself to sleep, which you already know. I hold long conversations with you when I'm alone, which you also know. But being here...." She faltered, and then tried again. "I know you're always with me, but being here...." Her voice splintered. "I feel like you're standing next me."

A blue jay flapped its wings as it flew over them.

Grace looked up. "Is that you?"

Another round of tears swept through them all.

The bird flew back where it had initially come from.

"I'm taking that as a yes." Grace sniffed. "I told you about Cody and Isabella giving us a grandson, and that they're going to name him Brince. That's so incredible and special. I hope tiny Brince looks like you. I'm headed to Italy soon to be with our little family, and I'll smother them with love. There's something I have to ask you, Brince. It's difficult to find the right words. I played them over and over in my head all the way here. Actually,

I've been playing them in my head for weeks. It's finally time to say them." Grace looked at Elaina, Tawny, and Steph. Then she stared straight ahead. "I've found love again. With Philip. He's not you, Brince, but he makes me happy. He cares about Cody, Isabella, Karina, and our grandson. What I'm trying to ask, and going around the block several times with a lot of words instead of just putting it out there, is that I'd like your permission to ask Philip to marry me."

Elaina gave the side-eye to Tawny and Steph. Their mouths were ajar.

The blue jay squawked.

"Grace, I believe Brince approves."

Grace swayed and she was caught by her three best friends. She cried heavy tears until there were none left to fall. Getting her bearings, she asked if they could go somewhere for a stout cup of coffee.

In the car, Steph patted Grace through the opening in the headrest. "I love you, Grace."

"I love you too, Steph. And Elaina. And Tawny." Grace stretched her neck from side to side. "Now floor it. I need a jolt of caffeine in the worst way."

Elaina pulled into the first gas station that advertised coffee. "It might taste like mud or it might be awesome. Either way, it's going to happen."

Each with a large coffee, they set out again.

"Where to, sassy chicks?"

"We have a half an hour to kill before the bridal shop opens. Let's find Grady so Tawny can jump his bones." Steph said, "Oww," when Tawny punched her arm.

"I'm not going to jump his bones. I couldn't if I wanted to, he's at work. I'm going to stop in and ask how things are going."

Elaina looked in the rearview mirror. "Should you let him know you're coming?"

"And ruin the element of surprise?"

Elaina raised her eyebrows in the mirror for Tawny to see. "It's another test. You want to see how he reacts to your unexpected presence."

"You always have a feel for what I'm thinking and what I'm going to do next."

"Kinda scary, huh?"

"It's all good."

"I'll take that as a compliment. Now direct me to Grady's office."

Across town, they came to a parking lot filled with vehicles, not an empty space was to be found.

Tawny pointed to a shiny black Chevy. "That's Grady's car."

Steph asked if they should smear the handles with axle grease.

Elaina nixed that plan right out of the gate. "We don't keep axle grease on hand and Grace didn't bring her catwoman mask."

"Yes I did." Grace pulled it out of her purse.

"Good thing the TSA agent at the airport didn't search your purse." Tawny heckled Grace a little bit more. "The underwear and mask would've drawn a laugh or earned you a trip to the private area where they strip search."

Elaina reached her hand back for Tawny to smack.

"Get out of the car, circus monkey," Grace ordered.

Tawny glared. No doubt she'd retaliate when she got the chance.

"Do you want us to wait here for you?"

Steph mentioned seeing a dollar store down the street.

"I guess we're going to shop. Text when you're ready for us to come back."

Tawny ambled up the sidewalk to a door marked 'Employees Only'. She turned and held up her hand to show crossed fingers.

Elaina lowered the window. "You've got this, woman."

Tawny pressed a buzzer and someone came to let her in.

Steph changed her mind about the dollar store and wanted to visit the drugstore across from it, instead.

The second they stepped inside, the clerk offered assistance.

Without cracking a smile, Steph asked where they could locate personal lubrication.

The clerk also kept a straight face and directed them to the end of aisle nine.

Steph took a shopping basket. "Thank you. We have to stock up."

Elaina jiggled with a laugh, but she didn't lose it until Grace said, "She goes through that stuff like it's toothpaste."

* * *

Steph held up a box of condoms. "It says they're ultra-sensitive. Does that mean they cry easily?"

Grace didn't get the joke or she was embarrassed. She batted Steph's hand down. "How would I know? I don't work here."

"You're on a roll, Steph. Have fun. I'll be over there, rummaging through the Easter clearance bin." Elaina's phone plinked with an incoming text. "It's only been eleven minutes. Surely you can't be ready for us to come back this soon."

Instead of a message from Tawny, she'd received one from Chad. She located Grace and Steph. "I'm going outside to call Chad."

Grace made kissing noises.

"Yeah, we might do some virtual-smooching"

The sun shone brightly, warming the spring air. Elaina propped against the car to soak up some natural Vitamin D.

Chad answered on the first ring. "Hello, beautiful. How's your day so far?"

"Interesting."

"In a good way, I hope."

"Definitely good. How about yours?"

"Also good. I took coffee and donuts to the guys. Are we still on for lobster tonight?"

Elaina went slack. "Oops. I completely forgot. I'm in Ohio right now."

He didn't sound angry, just surprised. "Ohio?"

She explained how she happened to be in the buckeye state and then borrowed his words from last night. "Hands down, I made time for my besties."

"Touché. That makes you a keeper."

They talked for another ten minutes.

Elaina's phone chimed – Tawny was ready for pickup.

Grace and Steph walked out of the drugstore with laughter rolling off them.

"I have to go. We'll be home late tonight. If you're available tomorrow, we could do lobster rolls and crab – my treat."

"I just want to see you. Call me when you're free. Until then, have fun with those ornery girls. See you, sweetheart."

"By the pleased look on your face, I get the feeling things are heating up with Officer Chad. You might need some of this." Grace plucked a tube of lube from the drugstore bag and threw it to Elaina.

"You should keep this, Grace. It'll expire before it gets used."

"Get real. You can't keep your hands off each other. You'll need another tube by the end of the week."

* * *

Bursting with excitement, Tawny tossed her purse in the car and did some seat-dancing. "He loves me. Why couldn't it have been this good the first time around?"

"Ert. Then you wouldn't have met us."

"You're so right, Grace. I never would've found my BFF's. It boils down to a case of pain for a lot of gain." Tawny went on and on about Grady kissing her and getting handsy in his cubicle. "He has four days left to work and then he's all mine. The realtor's coming tonight to get the paperwork signed and then the house will officially be up for sale. After the realtor leaves, Grady's going to call Bo and Quentin to give them the news."

"How do you think they'll react?"

"They'll be shocked, kind of like I still am. Pinch me so I know this is real."

Steph nipped Tawny's arm.

"Dang it, Steph. It was a figure of speech."

"I'm a literal person. If you say pinch me, I'm happy to oblige. Driver, take me to the bridal store." Steph playfully wrinkled her nose. "Tawny Pia, Grace Viv' has something for you."

Grace handed Tawny a package with eight wine charms. "There are four beads on each charm – they represent the members of the No Sweat Pants Allowed – Wine Club."

"Us," Steph added.

"She gets wine charms and I get lube?"

"Don't get your panties in a bunch." Grace reached into the bag a second time. " Instead of a regular size tube of lubricant, she dropped one that said 'Fifty-percent more' in Tawny's lap.

"Ultra-sensitive. Fifty-percent more. I'll bet you had a coupon too." Elaina broke into a full-body laugh, making it difficult to keep her foot steady on the gas pedal. "I don't think I've laughed this much all month." She was still yukking it up when they got to the bridal shop.

Steph grabbed hold of the fancy doorknob to the shop. "I'm counting on you to keep me calm. I'm the happiest woman ever; I'm also ready to chew my fingernails to the quick." There was a notable tremble in her voice. "The last wedding dress I bought, I had to return."

"Buying another wedding dress won't bring bad luck."

"Tawn', don't make fun of me."

"I'm not, Steph. I just don't want you to compare what happened with Corbett-the-snake to what's going on with Nick. In the cruelest of ways, the snake did you a favor. He slithered out, making way for your true soul mate."

"You're right. I can't let the past mess with my future." Steph half-hugged Tawny.

"We're all guilty of letting the hurt back in. We have to stop doing that. One word says it all: forward."

"You're so wise, Tawny."

"I meant the only way to get in the shop is to move our feet forward."

Steph backhanded Tawny on the arm.

Two dresses called Steph's name – one in champagne, the other in eggshell. She tried on the champagne dress and twirled in front of the mirror. "What do you think?" Steph put her face in her hands. "I love it. But does it love me?"

She received a rousing round of "You look beautiful!"

"It complements your skin tone." Elaina also said it made Steph's green eyes pop.

Steph gnawed on her thumbnail.

"No nail chewing." Tawny held out her hand to show her fingernails. "As you know, I used to be a huge nail-biter. I hooked up with you gals and my nerves calmed.

Once in a while I get riled up, and I rip into a nail. Then I get ticked at myself for falling back on a nasty habit. Do you know how many germs live under your nails?"

"I don't know. A zillion?"

"Ding, ding. You got it right."

Grace pointed out that Tawny had also quit smoking.

"You've all been a blessing. I wish everyone going through hard times with their spouses or significant others could find a good friend – or three good friends – to help them get their footing."

Elaina thought she was all cried out. Turns out she was wrong. "You've been a blessing to us too, Tawn'. Don't forget that."

Grace sniffled.

Steph dug in her purse for a tissue and blew her nose.

Tawny swiped at the corners of her eyes. "We're such bawl babies. We freaking cry all the time."

Elaina said, "Crying keeps us from getting ulcers – and from biting our nails."

"Or we're just whiny-asses."

"Cordray, you're shock-entertainment."

Laughter dried up their tears.

The shop owner's expression was straight-up serious. She kept an eye on them. Elaina had done the same thing to her. Their antics would almost bring a smile, then the woman would catch herself and it wouldn't happen. She'd tilt her head, either in surprise or in annoyance – it was hard to tell. Elaina smiled to herself, acknowledging that the No Sweat Pants Allowed – Wine Club ladies made an impression wherever they went.

"Here's the second dress." Steph strutted across the floor in the viewing area like she was on a New York fashion runway. She smoothed her hand across the fabric. "Stephanie Irene Mathews-Augustine is wearing a silk floor-length dress in soft eggshell. The subtle gathers at the bodice makes her small chest look remarkable. The slit from the bottom of the dress to part way up her thigh, is so sexy that Nicholas Augustine will have to be reminded to keep his eyes on her face during the ceremony."

The owner had glued her ear to Steph's commentary and came to seal the deal. "You're gorgeous in that dress. You'll not find another that highlights your features the way this one does."

Steph posed several times in the mirror. "I haven't made a decision."

An compulsory smile creased the woman's lips. Fortunately, she shuffled away when another bride and her wedding party came in.

"Quick, Grace, grab a paper and pen, and write down the designer's names and bar codes for both dresses. I can't buy either dress here. I'd have to fly back for fittings."

Steph felt obliged to purchase something, so she bought a cake knife.

Grace sighed with contentment. "Tawny, Steph, and I have satisfied our reasons for coming to Ohio. Now it's your turn, Elaina. Are we visiting Rachel?"

"That wasn't the destination I had in mind." Elaina turned on the radio to a classic rock station. She eased the volume down so the music wouldn't interfere with their conversation. Donning a pair of sunglasses, she shoved the key in the ignition.

"What was I thinking?" Grace winced. "Where's there's Rachel, there's Arden. Seeing him again this soon might make your eyeballs fall out."

"Arden no longer has power over my eyeballs, or anything else." Elaina polled her passengers. "Visit Rachel? Yay or nay? Majority rules." Three nays, hers made four.

"What do you have up your sleeve? Are we working out at the gym you once owned?" Tawny flicked her tricep. "I need to lift weights to tone up."

"We'll do some curls, just not with hand weights."

"What does that even mean?"

"You'll see."

Main Street came into view. Elaina drove two city blocks and stopped the rental car in front of the jewelry store where they met.

Grace squealed with joy. "Leave it to you to think of everything! This makes the day perfect!"

"I thought we could do a walk-thru, for old time sake."

"Yes, yes," Tawny seconded.

Steph was out of the car and in the store before the others had their seatbelts unlatched.

The jeweler recognized Elaina immediately. They'd been members of the Chamber of Commerce together for a number of years.

"Good to see you, Elaina."

"It's nice to see you too, Pete."

"I heard you sold out and moved to Maine."

"It's a beautiful state. Should you find yourself in Portland and in need of a place to stay, the girls and I own a bed and breakfast. Steph makes a mean omelet."

"I'll keep you in mind." The small talk ran out. "Did you gals come in for something specific?"

Tawny crouched to ogle shimmering wedding sets. "We're here to celebrate our ten-month anniversary."

"We have a great selection of gifts ideal for any anniversary."

Elaina asked about charms that said sister.

"Follow me." He walked to the opposite end of the store and spun a rotating display that held charms galore. "I only have one style in the sister charm. I hope you'll find it to your liking."

Elaina studied the small sterling-silver piece of jewelry. "What do you think?"

"It's a must-have." Grace inquired if Pete had four charms on hand.

He searched the drawer below the display. "I have exactly four."

Grace had her credit card at the ready. "These are on me."

"We can buy our own."

"No. I want to get these. If you hadn't tuned into my tears that day, I'd still be a miserable wretch. Instead, the three of you helped me through a very difficult time. Basically, you bandaged my broken heart with your friendship."

"We'll need chains too." Elaina footed the bill for them.

Tawny anchored her hands on her hips. "What can I pay for?"

Steph took her wallet out of her purse. "What about me? I have to pay for something."

Elaina pointed to the bar across the street. "Tawny and Steph, we'll let you buy us a glass of wine."

"Just a glass?"

"Unless you want to put that extra pair of underwear to good use, we have to limit our intake to one."

Pete looked confused.

Elaina shook his hand, instead of explaining that too much wine would hinder their return to the airport and subsequent flight home.

In the bar, Tawny led them to the exact table where they'd poured out their stories.

The same spiky-haired, tight-jeans wearing bartender rushed to greet them. His eyes flickered with recognition. "Ladies, it's been a while."

Tawny spoke for them when she said, "We've been busy." Different from the last time, she didn't roam her eyes over every yummy inch of him.

He cocked a sexy eyebrow. "I remember calling a cab. You girls were hammered. Good times, right?"

"It was the night that changed our lives." Instead of offering more, Steph scanned the wine menu.

He searched their faces. "For the better?"

"Damn skippy," Grace clucked.

"You were here to celebrate something. What was it?"

"Friendship." Grace yanked the wine menu away from Steph.

"That's as good a reason as any to get toasted." His gaze skimmed over Elaina, and settled on Tawny's chest.

Tawny mumbled under her breath, "Some things never change." She raised her cheeks in a confident, high-smile. "I'm taken."

Elaina was quick to say, "Me too."

Grace and Steph followed suit.

Someone across the bar shouted that they wanted another Jack and coke, prompting the bartender to circle back to the business at hand. "Have you decided what you'd like to drink?"

Tawny ordered a bottle of blackberry wine. "It's Elaina's favorite."

"We don't have to drink what I like."

"Yes we do. Because of you, life is great."

The bartender's curiosity was piqued even more. "What did she do?"

Steph smiled at Elaina. "There aren't enough hours in the day to list all the kindnesses she's extended to us."

"Cool, dude."

Grace informed him they weren't dudes.

"I call everyone dude."

Tawny acted the fool by clutching her neck and making raspy throat noises.

"I should probably get the wine."

"Geez. I thought he'd never leave." Tawny dug the wine charms out of her purse.

Elaina stretched out her arms and laid her hands on the table. The others did the same so their fingers touched. "I love you ladies.

"We love you more."

The bartender returned, popped the cork on the bottle, and filled their glasses. Tawny snapped on the wine charms.

"You brought your own bling?"

"The last time we were here, we brought along some serious bling – wedding rings we wanted to dispose of. So yeah," Steph said cockily, "we're known to bring the bling."

He shuttered his lashes as though he didn't quite believe everything they said.

Grace set the record straight. "You may think we hit the hooch before we came in. You'd be wrong. We're not yet under the influence of alcohol, we're just weird." She cracked up at her own witty remark.

Tawny asked if *We Are Family* by Sister Sledge was on the jukebox. It was the song they'd sang karaoke to, and the song everyone sang at Cody and Isabella's wedding reception.

"I'm not sure. I'll check." The bartender fixed his attention on the necklace-charm setting above Tawny's cleavage.

"We all have one." Steph held out her necklace.

"We're sisters," Elaina joyfully proclaimed.

His look of doubt returned. "You look nothing alike."

Elaina raised her glass in the air. "We've had an extraordinary ten months. Here's to a hundred years."

Tawny, Steph, and Grace clinked their glasses against Elaina's.

"Good things are happening, ladies. What exactly the

future holds for us though, is unknown. Only one thing will remain clear and steady through it all – we're wine sisters forever!"

~ The End ~

I'm sad to end this series, but it's time to say goodbye to Elaina, Tawny, Steph, and Grace. They've been a big part of my life for a few years and have given me a lot of joy. I hope as you've read their stories that you smiled or laughed a little.

Thank you from the bottom of my heart for sticking with these characters, while they formed lasting friendships and searched for ways to deal with their new circumstances.

~ Jan

About the Author

Jan Romes grew up in northwest Ohio in the midst of eight zany siblings. Married to her high school sweetheart for more years than seems possible, she's also a mom, mother-in-law, and grandma.

Jan writes contemporary romance and women's fiction with sharp, witty characters who give as good as they get. The more she writes the more risk she's willing to take with her characters.

When she's not writing, you can find Jan with her nose buried in a book or engaged in some sort of activity to stay fit. She loves spending time with family and friends. A hopeless romantic, she loves music, enjoys sunsets, gets teary-eyed in over sappy movies, and stares into a campfire every chance she gets.

Though she doesn't claim to have a green thumb, she grows flowers and pumpkins.

Jan loves to hear from her readers and is passionate about discussing everything about writing. So don't be shy. Jan.romes@yahoo.com

You can follow Jan here:

Website:	www.authorjanromes.com
Blog:	www.jantheromancewriter.blogspot.com
Twitter:	www.twitter.com/JanRomes
Facebook:	www.facebook.com/jan.romes5
Goodreads:	www.goodreads.com/author/show/5240156.Jan_Romes
Amazon:	www.amazon.com/Jan-Romes/e/B005OMZICY

Other books by Jan Romes

Texas Boys Falling Fast series:
Book #1 – Married to Maggie
Book #2 – Keeping Kylee
Book #3 – Taming Tori
Book #4 – Not Without Nancy

Single-title books:
One Small Fib
Lucky Ducks
Kiss Me
The Gift of Gray
Stay Close, Novac!
Stella in Stilettos
Three Wise Men
The Christmas Contract
Mr. August
Three Days with Molly
Big on Christmas
I'd Rather Be Growing Grapes
Wild Goose Chase
Tucked Away
Loving Lindy
Two More Miles
The Great Mistletoe Project

Wine and Sweat Pants series:
Book #1 - No Sweat Pants Allowed – Wine Club
Book #2 - Sipping Sangria
Book #3 - Merlot in Maine
Book #4 - Wine Club Wednesdays
Book #5 - Wine Sisters Forever

Made in United States
Troutdale, OR
04/08/2025

30443398R00151